DOUBLE TOIL AND TROUBLE

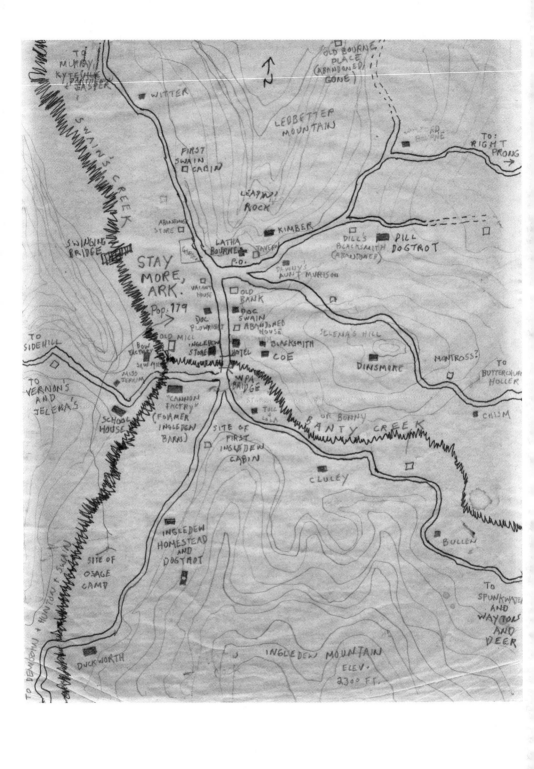

DOUBLE TOIL AND TROUBLE

A NEW NOVEL AND SHORT STORIES
BY DONALD HARINGTON

EDITED BY BRIAN WALTER

The University of Arkansas Press | Fayetteville

2020

Frontispiece:
Hand-drawn map of Stay More by Donald Harington.

ISBN: 978-1-68226-142-2
eISBN: 978-1-61075-727-0

Manufactured in the United States of America

24 23 22 21 20   5 4 3 2 1

♾ The paper used in this publication meets the minimum
requirements of the American National Standard for Permanence
of Paper for Printed Library Materials Z39.48-1984.

Library of Congress Cataloging-in-Publication Data
Names: Harington, Donald, author. | Walter, Brian, 1966– editor.
Title: Double toil and trouble / a new novel and short stories
by Donald Harington; edited by Brian Walter.
Description: Fayetteville: The University of Arkansas Press, 2020. |
Summary: "Double Toil and Trouble is a posthumous volume of
fiction by Arkansas novelist Donald Harington (1935–2009).
Featuring a suspense novel and four stories, this collection adds
several new chapters to the saga of Stay More, the fictional Ozarks
village where Harington set more than a dozen novels."
—Provided by publisher.
Identifiers: LCCN 2020010038 (print) | LCCN 2020010039 (ebook) |
ISBN 9781682261422 (cloth; alk. paper) | ISBN 9781610757270 (ebook)
Classification: LCC PS3558.A6242 A6 2020 (print) |
LCC PS3558.A6242 (ebook) | DDC 813/.54—dc23
LC record available at https://lccn.loc.gov/2020010038
LC ebook record available at https://lccn.loc.gov/2020010039

CONTENTS

Acknowledgments

Everyone whom I have previously thanked for supporting my Harington-focused publications and productions certainly deserves more thanks for helping, in one way or the other, to make *Double Toil and Trouble* possible. This statement includes all of the friends, family, students, student assistants, colleagues, correspondents, kindly acquaintances, and personal inspirations whom I singled out in the voluminous (and joke-filled) credits of both *Stay More: The World of Donald Harington* and *Farther Along: The World of Donald Harington, Part 2* (University of Arkansas Press, 2013 and 2015, respectively); it also, inevitably, includes both those whom I thanked en masse and those whom I burdened with more personal effusions in *The Guestroom Novelist: A Donald Harington Miscellany* (University of Arkansas Press, 2019). Every fond, foolish idiot who turns a chunk of his life over to the cause of making a book should be so blessed in his village of supporters and well-wishers as I have been in these endeavors. A full roll call would swell Stay More beyond any limits that even its dear creator ever imagined for it, but it would, at the least, include the following (in alphabetical order): Deborah Meghnagi Bailey, Mike Bieker, Lori Birrell, Jennifer Harington Brizzi (hi, Sophia and Marco!), Kevin Brockmeier, Amie Brooks, Gale Messick Cantrell, David Chaudoir, D. S. Cunningham, Jeff Falzone, Dayton Ford, Janet Foxman (for conscientious editing), Melanie Griffin, Georgina Hamilton, Kim Harington (Harington's real-life Latha), Katie Herman (for scrupulous copy editing), Chris Herring, Jordan Hickey, Sherrie Hoffmann, Linda Hughes, Susan Kavanaugh, Kyle Kellams, Susan Kendrick-Perry, Melissa King, Mari Kurisato, Naomi Lebowitz, Liz Lester, Louis Maistros, Trey Marley, Philip Martin, Becca Martin-Brown, Bill "Papa on Permanent Vacation" McNamara, Abel Milgod, J. Brad Minnick, Tim Nutt, Deena Owens, Mike Patrick, Molly Bess Rector, Sam Ridge, Christian Saia, Arch Schaffer, Bill Schwab, Charlie Shields, Geoffery Stark, St. Louis College of Pharmacy, Peter Straub, Susan Rooker Tonymon, Brenda Walter (my very own Latha—and so, so much more), Lori Watson, Katrina Windon, and Beth Withey and the Ozarks Chorale.

There's one more person who deserves a special expression of gratitude in this volume. Angela Doerr, our redoubtable resident dramaturge and Steve Rogers connoisseur, not only transformed my dodgy PDF of *Double Toil and Trouble* (complete with Louie Howland's faint, decades-old emendations) into a functional Microsoft Word file for my editorial efforts; she also provided invaluable reassurance of this project's viability when she returned the manuscript to me wide-eyed and announced, "I didn't see *that* ending coming!" Please blame any errors that made it into this published version on yours truly, not her.

Brian Walter, St. Louis, April 2, 2020

Grand Schemes

"Louie may have told you of his Grand Scheme for licking
the jinx that hovers over me. As a result, I'm now writing a
'deliberately unambitious divertissement,' a thriller. The critics won't
know what to make of it. Neither will I, for that matter."
—Donald Harington, 1973

A S IT TURNED OUT, both critics and fans of Donald Harington's work would have to wait almost half a century before getting a chance to make something of the diverting thriller in question. Harington wrote *Double Toil and Trouble* during the first few months of 1973 in response to a vague but compelling request by Llewellyn "Louie" Howland III, his still rather new editor at Little, Brown, for a "novel that quite deliberately adheres to the traditional modes of conventional fiction . . . a neatly plotted, tightly drawn divertissement."[1] That last word, *divertissement*, shows up several more times in Harington's subsequent letters of 1973, when he refers (with ironic self-deprecation) to the story of Hock Tuttle and the mysterious Mrs. Wilson, a woman "just this side of middle-aged" who is "dressed city-style but not expensively" when she shows up in the first chapter at the train station in Hock's hometown of Pettigrew, Arkansas. As Mrs. Wilson soon learns, Pettigrew is as close as she can get by rail to her intended destination, the remote, rugged, and entirely fictional Ozark village of Stay More, which Harington had first created a few years earlier for his 1970 novel, *Lightning Bug*, and which would provide the setting for (or figure prominently in) the subsequent twelve novels he would publish over the ensuing four decades. Mrs. Wilson's errand to Stay More seems as unsettling as it is urgent, revolving

---

1. From Louie Howland's January 5, 1973, letter to Harington. For more information about this letter and other contexts for *Double Toil and Trouble*, please see the appendix below, "A Deliberately Unambitious Divertissement."

around a pair of large oblong pine boxes that are "tapered out to their widest point at the place where a body's shoulders might be" and marked with but a single letter each. With no other wheeled transport available, Hock offers his wagon and mules for the final leg of Mrs. Wilson's journey, innocently entangling himself in what will turn out to be a mystery unlike any other in the Stay More canon.

At just under 37,000 words, *Double Toil and Trouble* (or *DUB*, following Harington's custom of using handy three-letter abbreviations for his books) is easily the shortest of the Stay More novels. *DUB* stands out in Harington's work in other ways as well: the unusual Shakespearean title, the relatively strict third-person perspective, and—perhaps most curiously—the lack of any verb tense shifts in the concluding chapters.[2] Harington wrote *DUB* in the midst of his work on what he would come to call "the Bible of Stay More," his 1975 novel, *The Architecture of the Arkansas Ozarks* (or *TAOTAO*), which devotes several chapters to the third generation of Ingledews (Stay More's founding family), which *DUB* focuses its entirety on. But where *TAOTAO* takes a macroscopic view of the history of Stay More, covering some 160 years in the course of its twenty chapters, *DUB* contents itself with a comparative microcosm, devoting its thirteen chapters to the span of about a week.

To learn more about the backstory of this previously unpublished installment in the Stay More saga, please see the appendix below, "A Deliberately Unambitious Divertissement," where selections from Harington's correspondence from the period clearly demonstrate the author's disappointment that it was not published at the time. In fact, as his letters to *DUB*'s dedicatee, Dick McDonough, particularly make clear, Harington envisaged the novel's publication someday even after Howland had declined it. The publisher's grand scheme had worked for the author, at any rate.

If *DUB* itself represents the grandest of the grand schemes presented in this volume, the stories that follow it—spanning some three decades of Harington's career—spring no less eagerly from the same hope for a

---

2. All of Harington's other books (including his 1986 nonfiction novel, *Let Us Build Us a City*) shift from the past to the present and, finally, to the future tense to (in effect) conclude the book without ending the story. (See *The Guestroom Novelist: A Donald Harington Miscellany*, especially pp. 132 and 173, for Harington's explanation of his signature narrative strategy; see also the final paragraphs of his final novel, 2009's *Enduring*.)

wider readership. The first two represent Harington's *"Esquire* period," the middle to late 1960s—between his first published novel, *The Cherry Pit* (1965), and *Lightning Bug*—when his agent managed to place several stories in *Esquire*. Known for its complicated prescription of masculine lifestyles in midcentury America, the magazine had published Arthur Schlesinger's famous essay "The Crisis of American Masculinity" in the November 1958 issue and featured numerous writers—from Ernest Hemingway to Norman Mailer—whose work, often notoriously, spoke to both men's aspirations and their fears.[3] But regardless of their gender-inflected elements, both of the *Esquire* stories included here preview important themes and effects in Harington's later novels.

"A Second Career" offers Harington's take on an instructively standard figure in American literature: the man of the cloth who fails to practice what he preaches. Ambitious but unimaginative, especially in his interactions with women, Reverend Winstead displays unhealthy, even immature preoccupations that do not augur well for his calling. Similar traits mark out the preachers who will soon begin to show up in Harington's Stay More, including the ardent Every Dill in *Lightning Bug*, the magical Long Jack Stapleton (an unmistakable Harington avatar) in *The Architecture of the Arkansas Ozarks*, the uproariously hypocritical roosterroach Reverend Chiddiock Tichborne in *The Cockroaches of Stay More* (1989), and the obsessive, mean-spirited Emmett Binns of *The Pitcher Shower* (2005). But if Reverend Winstead seems like a mere stripling (both as an actor within his fictional world and as a character in Harington's pantheon) next to these more imposing successors, the efforts of this early story's would-be fictionist to ground his work in real, lived experience still allow the metafictionist in Harington to evoke the inevitable subjectivity of art, the inability of the final work *not* to embed a self-portrait of the artist. The struggling, self-obsessed young minister strives to blend reality meaningfully and essentially into his fictions, a key theme for Harington that would grow only more urgent as he elaborated it through his subsequent novels.

"Down in the Dumps" also makes itself an ironic heir to an important American literary tradition: the disillusioned insider's critique of

---

3. For a much fuller picture of *Esquire*'s complicated contributions to twentieth-century images and conventions of masculinity, see Brad Congdon's *Leading with the Chin: Writing American Masculinities in* Esquire, *1960–1989* (University of Toronto Press, 2018).

soul-killing materialism. Attorney Russell Thornhill gradually but deci-
sively grows more alienated from his career and his marriage in a scenario
that could easily turn tragic. But in Harington's hands, Thornhill's fall
works just as well as a comedic ascent to unexpected moral and philosophical freedoms. In fact, within the unlikely bromance that takes bloom in
the local junkyard, Harington conjures a possibility perhaps unique in all
of his fiction: a happy ending that does not spring from a hopeful coupling
between man and woman.

The other two stories selected for this collection jump forward a few
decades to the mid-1990s, when our author was facing the prospect of
losing his longtime publisher, Harcourt Brace & Company.[4] In a letter to
his editor dated June 22, 1995, Harington explained that he was enclosing
several slightly modified chapters from his forthcoming novel, *Butterfly
Weed* (1996), for submission to mainstream literary magazines and that,
with a "rekindled interest in the short story as a form," he intended "to
spend the rest of the summer trying to write a few new ones." The effort
didn't entirely work, at least not as the author had hoped; none of the stories were accepted at those literary magazines, and *Butterfly Weed* would,
in fact, prove the last Harington novel that Harcourt would publish. But
these labors did result in a pair of delightful stories, "Telling Time" and
"The Freehand Heart," that both underscore the importance of Stay
More to Harington's gifts as a creator of narrative fiction and show how
lovingly Harington had broadened the imaginative possibilities for his
Gentle Reader over his decades of novelist's work.

"Telling Time" tells the story of storytelling in Stay More, the child
Dawny from *Lightning Bug* (and, eventually, from Harington's 1998 novel,
When Angels Rest) sharing a winning tale of rival yarn spinners Lion (or,
really, Lyin') Jude and Harry Tongue (the first name a creative anagram
of "Donald" and the second a close reconfiguration of "Harington"). The
narrator of "Telling Time" is a classic Harington avatar, an aged, scholarly
version of the ardent young Dawny remembering how, as a child, he ate
up the very different types of stories that the rivals produced (Lion Jude
conjures fantastical fairy tales while Harry Tongue sticks to factual his-
torical creations). When Dawny declares a winner (or at least his personal
favorite) and proceeds to explain why, the child's innocent comparison

4. Beginning with his 1986 nonfiction novel, *Let Us Build Us a City*, Harington published five consecutive books with Harcourt, his longest continuous run with any of
his publishers.

of the storytellers' respective merits conveys some of the aged novelist's cleverest (and most wistful) commentary on his own work. Harington also uses the story to pay tribute to Mary Celestia Parler, a beloved folklorist and his predecessor as a member of the University of Arkansas faculty.[5] Within this clever scenario, "Telling Time" touches deftly on the deepest, most heartfelt themes of the world of Stay More: the hungry imagination; the bountiful, complex relationship among language, nature, and identity; and the yearning for love and human connection.

The final entry of the volume, "The Freehand Heart," perhaps surpasses even "Telling Time" in its masterful layering of signature Harington themes. If, at first, the relationship that develops between the two protagonists, Richard "Dick" Roe and Omega "Meg" Koontz, seems like little more than a sweet coming-of-age romance between a clumsy country bumpkin and a lonely urban sophisticate transplanted to the hinterlands, Harington subtly builds it into something much more resonant by the end of the story. Bonded initially by their mockable names, Dick Roe and Meg Koontz find Stay More both bringing them together and testing their relationship in ways that they could never have anticipated. The title of this cleverly deromanticized romance by itself suggests Harington's munificent loneliness as an artist, and the story it heads cleverly realizes the ambition of inscribing one's name into nature. The story ends with a revelation that may seem like a mistake but that finally helps "The Freehand Heart" to conjure an unusual vision of the fiercely independent artist—no matter how lonely the work.

Note on the Texts

As in the Harington-authored texts featured in *The Guestroom Novelist: A Donald Harington Miscellany* (University of Arkansas Press, 2019), I have tried to keep my editorial intrusions to a minimum in this volume, mostly correcting typos (and other obvious errors) and regularizing punctuation throughout. But where, in *The Guestroom Novelist*, the latter

---

5. Parler's students nicknamed her "Mrs. Chaucer" for her love of the medieval English poet whose inspired comedic treatment of vernacular speech serves as a precursor to Harington's own fascination, some six centuries later, with the inexhaustible delights of dialect. See "Mary Celestia Parler (1904–81)," CALS Encyclopedia of Arkansas, Central Arkansas Library System, last modified May 10, 2018, https://encyclopediaofarkansas.net/entries/mary-celestia-parler-3616/.

effort mostly involved the addition of Oxford commas that Harington sometimes left out, here in *DUB*, it has required the much more frequent excision of grammatically superfluous commas, particularly those that Harington oddly insisted on inserting between the elements of simple compound verbs. (Let me take a moment here to offer special thanks to copy editor Katie Herman for her diligent efforts to regularize the punctuation of this volume—at least to the degree that seemed safe in light of Harington's many creative idiosyncrasies as a writer.) Readers who would like to track the evolution of Harington's usage practices across the decades are strongly encouraged to go through the original typescript of *DUB*, which is available in the Harington archive maintained by the University of Arkansas's Special Collections.

The original typescript of *DUB* should also prove a boon to anyone interested in Harington's always-complicated relationship with editors and the publishing business. The typescript retains editor Louie Howland's often detailed critiques, suggestions, and corrections penciled into the margins and within the text itself. Initially, I planned to include these annotations in footnotes, but I soon abandoned the idea, primarily because Harington's ghost almost immediately forsook its cozy haunts in Stay More to charge my desk chair in St. Louis and howl in protest at the outrageous idea of intruding on the reader's experience with such needless, distracting trivia. So, while it seems likely (had they ended up seeing *DUB* into print together) that Harington would have accepted several of the more minor edits that Howland suggested, it also seemed best in this case to present a version that sticks as faithfully to the author's original vision as possible.

DOUBLE TOIL
AND TROUBLE

A NOVEL BY

DONALD HARINGTON

To Dick McDonough

HECATE. O! well done! I commend your pains,
And every one shall share i' the gains.
And now about the cauldron sing,
Like elves and fairies in a ring,
Enchanting all that you put in.
MACBETH, III 6

CHAPTER 1

Young Hock Tuttle was sweeping the platform one morning when the twice-weekly train from Fayetteville came steaming slowly into the sleepy village of Pettigrew, the end of its line. Hock quickly finished sweeping and returned his broom to the station. He watched the brakeman disconnect the engine couplings so the engineer could shuttle the big steam locomotive around to the rear of the train to pull it back to Fayetteville. Hock liked to watch these small men manipulating such huge pieces of machinery.

"Hey, Hawk!" A man in the door of the freight car motioned him to come over. "Give me a hand."

In the door of the freight car were two long wooden boxes, made of sanded pine, identical boxes, each over six feet long. The sides of the boxes were not parallel but tapered out to their widest point at the place where a body's shoulders might be. One by one, Hock helped the man lower them to the platform, grunting with the weight of them. Hock judged the contents must be adult and probably male. The coffins were plain but not cheap; they looked as if they had been handcrafted by a cabinetmaker. They had no labels or tags; there was no writing on the boxes except, inconspicuously in the corner of the side of each, a letter: *M* on one, *D* on the other.

"Where do I send 'em?" Hock asked.

"They aint freight," the man said. "It's baggage." He nodded his head toward the other end of the train where, Hock saw, the sole passenger, a woman, had just stepped down from the train. She began walking toward the coffins. The man climbed back into the freight car and left Hock alone with the coffins and the woman.

She was just this side of middle-aged, Hock figured. It isn't easy for a young man of twenty to know whether an older woman is thirty or fifty. She didn't have any wrinkles, but there were a couple of wisps of gray among the short blond hairs that sneaked out the bottom of her hat. She was dressed city-style but not expensively and was carrying an old leather suitcase along with her purse and parasol. A little bit on the plump side, Hock thought, but not at all a bad looker.

"Well," she said to him, "is this Pettigrew?"

"Yes'm," he replied and wondered if the woman was too bereaved to notice the signs of "Pettigrew" clearly attached to the face and sides of the station.

"And the train won't go any farther?" she asked.

"Caint," he said. "Track ends here."

The woman turned and stared at the end of the track and then at the gentle mountains beyond, to the east. She turned back. "Are you the stationmaster?" she asked.

"More or less," he said.

"Could you tell me how far it is to Stay More?"

He studied it. "Why, that's clean over in the next county," he told her. "A right fur ways over."

"How long would it take me to get there?" she asked, and added, "With these": the two coffins.

"You aim to git a motor truck?" he asked.

"If I could," she said.

Sherm Crawford had the only truck that he knew of, or the only truck for hire, and Sherm lived half a mile out on the Muddy Gap Road. Hock didn't even know if the roads between here and Stay More were good enough for a motor truck. He'd heard there was some pretty wild country up around in there. But Sherm seemed to be the only one to ask.

"Wal, let me tend to a couple of things, and then I'll see if I caint find ye one," Hock said to the woman. "You kin set inside the station."

"I'll sit here," she said, and sat on one of the coffins, the one marked *D*.

Hock finished his chores at the station, then carried two sacks of mail over to the post office. "That all the train brung?" the postmistress asked him.

"Gits lighter ever time," Hock observed.

He walked on out to Sherm Crawford's house on Muddy Gap Road. The truck wasn't in sight, but Clovena Crawford was sitting on the front porch, churning butter.

"Howdy, Miz Crawford," he said. "Sherm home?"

"Noo, he's done went to Huntsville with a load of sheep. I don't 'spect to see him back before the weekend."

"Aw," Hock remarked in disappointment. "They's a lady down to the station has two coffins and wants to be drove over to Stay More in Newton County."

"Who's in the coffins?"

"She didn't say."

"Wal, don't Tim Brashear have a truck?"

"Yeah, but two of the tars is bad, and he don't have ere a spare."

"Hhmmm," said Clovena Crawford. "Reckon she'll jist have to wait till Sherm gits back, 'less she don't mind a ordinary wagon."

Hock walked back into town and told the woman that there weren't any trucks available. "How big a hurry are you in?" he asked and realized that didn't sound too polite to a possibly grieving mother or daughter or sister or niece or whatever she was. "I mean, did you want to git on up there today, or could you wait around a while?"

"The sooner, the better" was all she would say.

"They won't keep, huh?" Hock said, indicating the coffins, but realized that was an awful thing to say.

"They'll keep," the woman said. "They're embalmed."

"Oh," Hock said. He wasn't sure what *embalmed* meant, but it sounded like it had something to do with preserving them. When somebody around Pettigrew died, folks got him into the ground as fast as they could.

"I kin git holt of a team and wagon, if that aint too slow fer ye," he offered. Actually, he'd been thinking about setting his cap for Viola Haskins that evening, but she could wait, and he could use whatever money he could get for it.

"All right," she said. "Now?"

"In a couple of winks," he said. Hock's house wasn't far from the station, just up the hill a way. He walked home at a brisk clip and harnessed his two mules and hitched them to the wagon. He climbed up and drove to the porch of his house, where his mother was standing. "Whar ye off to, boy?" she asked.

"They's a lady with two coffins down to the station wants to be drove plumb over to Stay More in Newton County," he said.

"Huh?" his mother said. "Who's in the coffins?"

"Darn if I know," he said. "I never ast her."

"Wal, you won't git back before sundown or even tomorrow," she said. "Hold on a minute and let me fix you somethin."

Hock waited while his mother hurried around in the kitchen and came back with a sack full of food and a half-gallon jar of milk. "She aim to pay you right well?" his mother asked.

"I never ast her," Hock said. Then, "Look fer me when you see me," he said with a smile and drove back to the station. The train had pulled out on its way back to Fayetteville, so he drove his wagon out onto the tracks and up alongside the platform to where the coffins were. The platform was high enough that he could slide and tilt each coffin up into the wagon without asking the woman for any help. There was just enough room in the wagon for the two coffins to rest side by side. "Okay," Hock said to the woman. "We kin go." He gave her his hand to assist her up onto the seat of the wagon, then he sat beside her, clucked at his mules, and they were off.

Hock hoped he could handle the journey without any trouble. He figured there wouldn't be any swollen streams to cross; in this time of June, all the creeks were low, hardly ever above the hubs.

But the road was rough, and his wagon had no springs. The seat they sat upon had springs, but these didn't do much to cushion the worse jolts. It was not long before Hock noticed that the woman was not enjoying the ride at all. She was trying to clutch her purse with one hand and hold on to the wagon seat with the other and not doing a very good job of either. Her face was pale, and her eyes looked pained, and she was gritting her teeth.

"I kin turn back," he offered. "The road's worse than I figgered."

"No," she said. "Go on."

They rode in silence for a while before the woman asked him, "What's your name?"

"Hawk Tuttle," he said. "What's yours?"

"Mrs. Wilson," she said. She is not going to get familiar, Hock decided. That was just as well. He had no particular curiosity about her. She was a live body whom he was transporting along with two dead bodies; whether or not they were also Wilsons, he did not really care. After he got her to Stay More, he would more than likely never see her again.

"Is that a nickname?" she asked.

"Which?"

"'Hawk,'" she said. "Like the bird."

"Naw, that's jist the way it's said," Hock told her.

After a few more miles in silence, she asked, "How old are you?"

"Twenty, ma'am," he replied, and before he could stop himself, he asked, "How old are you?"

"You aren't supposed to ask that," she said.

"Yeah," he said. "'Scuse me."

The road eastward as far as Red Star is uphill nearly all the way, and the mules took long, slow steps to pull their load, and occasionally Hock had to remind them by lashing the reins against their backs. Red Star is at the watershed divide, the streams to the west flowing into the White

River, those to the east draining into the Buffalo. From Red Star onward, they would go mostly downhill.

The first small village they passed through was Boston. The woman asked him, "What place is this?" and he told her the name of it. "Was it named after the other one?" she wanted to know.

"Which other one?" he said.

"There's a Boston in New England," she said. "The largest city in New England."

Hock remembered hearing something about New England when he had studied geography back in school. It was way off on an ocean somewhere. He wondered if the woman was from New England, but he didn't ask her.

A few people in Boston waved politely as they passed but then squinted their eyes and dropped their jaws to stare at the wagon with the unknown woman and the two coffins.

The woman noticed their stares. "I guess we *are* a sight," she observed.

"Yeah," Hock said. When they were outside the village, he opened the sack of food his mother had given him, took out ham and biscuit, and extended these to the woman. "Had your dinner yet?" he asked. She shook her head and thanked him and took the food and ate with him. He did not stop the wagon to eat, but he had to stop it to drink, passing the half-gallon jar of milk to the woman, who drank from it, and then drinking in his turn and driving on.

"That is good milk," the woman remarked. "Much richer than what we get in the city."

"It's good," he agreed. He'd spent some time seeing to it that the cow pasture was kept in good growth.

As the afternoon passed on, the woman asked, "Do you think we'll be there before dark?"

"I kinder doubt it," he said. He was getting into unfamiliar country now and would have to stop eventually and ask for directions. He did not know where Stay More is, exactly; he knew only that it is north of Swain and south of Jasper. If they could reach Fallsville by sundown, they'd be doing good.

"I would hate to have to spend the night with those," the woman said, indicating the coffins.

Hock looked at her. "Didn't you, last night?"

"On the train," she said. "But they were in the baggage car."

"Whar'd you come from?" he asked.

The woman laughed.

"I never meant that to be funny," he protested.

"No," she said, but laughed again. "It's just that you haven't asked me *any*thing. You aren't very nosy, are you?"

"I reckon not," he said. It was not that he wasn't nosy; he just didn't much care. He didn't care to know where she had come from, but since she was talking to him, he felt obliged to make talk.

"This is pretty country," she remarked. "And the air smells so fresh."

He had not noticed, but he said, "I reckon."

"Are you married?" she asked.

"Naw, I still live at home," he said, and would not need to return that question even if he cared, because she had already said she was *Mrs. Wilson.*

"Planning to be?" she asked.

"Sooner or later, I reckon," he said.

The next village they passed through was Red Star, and again, the woman asked him, "What place is this?" and when he told her the name of it, she asked, "Why is it called that?"

"I don't rightly know," he said. "It's always been called that." Again, people waved to them as they passed and squinted to see what cargo they were carrying.

There was a stretch of road east of Red Star that was very bad. Some of the holes and ruts were nearly hub deep, and although Hock slowed the mules and kept them reined, the wagon was jarred and tossed so much that the woman's face actually began to turn green. Suddenly, she cried, "Stop!" and as soon as he had stopped, she leapt down from the wagon and knelt beside the road and retched, upchucking all the ham and biscuit and milk she'd had for dinner. He went to her and laid his hand on the back of her neck; that was supposed to help. After a while, she rose to her feet and got a handkerchief from her purse and wiped her mouth with it. She looked at him as if to find some indication of his reaction to what she had done and then said, as if apologizing, "It wasn't the food. It was the ride. I'm all right now." She climbed back up into the wagon.

He drove very slowly thereafter, but she, noticing this, said, "It's all right now. The bumps won't bother me now. Let's get on." He drove a bit faster.

They came to a clearing at the crest of a hill, and a long panoramic sweep of hills in the Buffalo headwater country came into view. The woman gasped in delight and said, "It's beautiful! I've never been in this part of the country before." A short while later they were treated to a dazzling sunset, and the woman said, "Just look at that! This is really God's country!"

Hock was embarrassed at such displays of emotion and kept his eyes on the backs of the mules. He was aware that the woman sensed he wasn't sharing her sunset with her, and he mumbled, "Aw, shoot, I've seen better."

"You must have," she said. "You're very lucky, to live in this part of the country."

"Yeah, I guess so," he said, although he had never given it any thought, and more often than not, he figured that his luck was pretty bad sometimes in the long run.

"Tell me what Stay More is like," she requested.

"Never been there," he said.

"Oh. But you know how to get there?"

"More or less. Though when we git to Fallsville, I reckon I'd best find somebody to p'int out the right way."

They passed a house that had a sign tacked to an oak tree beside the road: "REEL LIMUN AID." The *E*s were backwards, Hock noticed. He wondered if Mrs. Wilson might like a drink if there was a bad taste in her mouth. He was a bit thirsty himself and very partial to lemonade when he could get it. He pointed the sign out to her and asked, "Keer fer any?"

She read the sign. "Lemonade?" she said. "I didn't know they grew lemons in this part of the country."

"They don't," Hock said. "But there's a fruit wagon passes through ever month or so." He stopped his wagon. The only person at the house was a man sitting on the porch. The man got up and came down to them. "Howdy," he said.

"Howdy," Hock replied. "Could we git us some lemonade?"

"Shore," the man said and returned to the porch, where he took two gourd dippers and stuck them into a crock and brought them out and gave one to each of them. Of course, there wasn't any ice in it, this time of the year, but it was made with cold springwater and was still pretty cold, and it was good.

"It's good stuff," Hock declared.

"Mmmm," Mrs. Wilson said, "yes."

The man noticed the two coffins in the wagon. "Whar you folks headin?" he asked.

"Stay More," Hock replied.

The man looked sorrowfully at Mrs. Wilson. "The Lord giveth and the Lord taketh away," he said. The man took off his hat and held it against his heart. "Over yonder in Glory the Lord has a Mansion a-waitin fer us."

Hock finished his lemonade in a few swallows.

"We'll all meet again on that beautiful shore in the sweet by-and-by," the man declared.

Mrs. Wilson finished her lemonade and returned the gourd dipper to the man.

"This world of sorrow and woe will be no more," the man said. "This time of toil and trouble will be fergot."

"That's mighty good lemonade," Hock declared. "How much we owe ye fer it?"

"Hit's usual a nickel," the man said, "but what is money in a time of sorrow? Let's us lay up our treasures in that home above."

Mrs. Wilson insisted on giving the man two nickels. As they drove away, the man said, "Jist lean on the Lord, sister!"

There were falls at Fallsville, and Hock stopped the wagon for a brief moment so the woman could admire the falls. Near the falls was a house, a cottage of cedar stained by the dampness and lack of light but looking well kept and loved by those who lived there, a family of three who were sitting on the porch enjoying the breeze after their supper. Hock stopped the wagon again. "Howdy," he said. "Could you folks tell us how to git towards Stay More?"

The father came down from the porch and with a stick drew a road map in the dust of the yard. "Take this here left prong when you come to Swain, and jist keep on it fer three mile."

One of the family, a small child, said, "Maw, what they got in them big boxes?"

The mother hushed the child and said, "Them's coffins, hon."

"With *dead* peop—?"

"*Sshhh!*" the mother said. "You hush now."

"I thank ye kindly," Hock said to the father and started the mules.

"Hold on!" the father said. "You'll never make it afore dark. Better jist stay the night with us."

Hock stopped the mules. He knew that such an invitation, even if wanted, must be declined twice, as a matter of proper formality, before being accepted. "We thank ye kindly," he said. "But we'd best be gittin on."

"No sense in that," the father said. "Unhitch the wagon and rest yore bones."

"We're obliged and beholden," Hock said, "but it's yet a while to dark."

"Time you'uns git up that hill yonder," the father said, "hit'll be too dark to see them mules' tails. Light down now, I say, and let's feed them critters."

"If we wouldn't be any bother," Hock said. He climbed down and went around the wagon to help Mrs. Wilson down. She seemed hesitant, or reluctant, and said quietly to him, "Where are we going to put the coffins?"

Under his breath, he replied, "Let's jist wait and see." To the father, he said, "Whar kin I put my wagon outa yore way?"

"Wherever you like. Put it in my barn, why don'tche?"

Hock looked at Mrs. Wilson. She asked, "Can he lock the barn?"

"I reckon not," Hock said. "Nobody never locks nothin hereabouts. But you aint worried they'll rise up and walk off, are ye?" The woman looked stricken, and he realized he had said possibly an unkind thing. "I mean, nobody'd wanter steal them coffins, would they?"

"I would simply feel better if—" she began.

"Tell ye what," Hock offered. "I'll sleep in the barn with 'em and keep my ear cocked."

She looked at him with awe, as if she doubted that anybody would dare do such a thing. Hock couldn't help but feel a little proud of his nerve. While he didn't exactly relish the idea of sleeping in the barn with dead people, it didn't frighten him in the slightest. Nothing, as far back as he could remember, had ever frightened him.

"You don't have to do that . . ." she protested.

"I don't keer," he said.

"Well, if you're sure . . ." she said.

Hock put the wagon in the barn, unhitched the mules, fed and watered them, twice declined the man's invitation to supper, and then accepted.

CHAPTER 2

The mother of the family, Hock discovered, was a Kissire and therefore a distant cousin of his own mother, although they had never met, and she hadn't been to Pettigrew in years, so Hock was kept up a good long while after supper filling her in on the whereabouts of all her Kissire kinfolk that he knew of.

Mrs. Wilson, after thanking their host and hostess and especially thanking Hock, said she was sleepy, so the mother of the family showed her upstairs to a bed, then came back downstairs full of questions for Hock. The family was disappointed that Hock knew practically nothing about the woman or the two dead persons. He tried to explain how he felt, or rather didn't feel, about it. It wasn't any of his business, he said. If Mrs. Wilson didn't want to tell him anything about who was in the coffins, she must have her reasons for it. And even if she did tell him who they were, it might not mean anything to him. He didn't know anybody in Stay More anyway.

The child came downstairs, complaining, "Maw, I caint sleep, thinkin a them coffins out to the barn."

"Shame on ye, chile," the father said. "This here feller aims to sleep right alongside them coffins. And if them bodies tries to rise up and come and git ye, ole Hawk'll stop 'em, won't ye, son?"

Hock nodded and said, "Shore thing. I'll not let 'em outa the barn."

The child looked at Hock with admiration and wonder and went back to bed.

The mother asked Hock, "What d'ye reckon she'll do when she gits to Stay More? Is she gonna bury 'em there and have you bring her on back to the train station?"

"Durn if I know," he said. "I didn't ast her."

"Didn't she even say whether you're hired for one way or round trip?" the father asked.

"Not that I kin remember," Hock said.

"Wal, how much is she payin you?" the father asked.

"She never said."

"How could two people die at the same time, I wonder?" the mother said.

"Could be they killed each other," the father observed.

"Or else somebody kilt 'em both," the mother said. "What do you think, Hawk?"

"Yeah," he admitted. "Could be one or both of 'em got killed." And then he said, "Reckon I'd best turn in. Much obliged to you'uns fer supper and fer puttin us up."

"You honestly fixin to sleep in the barn?" the mother asked.

"Shore," he said. "Aint it mighty bad luck to leave a corpse alone overnight?"

"That's shore a fact," she said. "Wal, let me git you a blanket and pillow."

Hock slept in the barn. The mules didn't seem to mind the coffins, so why should he? But he discovered, in his first efforts to fall asleep, that he couldn't help but speculate a while on the contents of the coffins. Were they male or female? Or one of each? The weight of the coffins would seem to indicate that they were both male, or else, if female, fat. Was one of them *Mr.* Wilson?

Hock almost went to sleep but then found himself playing a mental game with the letters *M* and *D* that were written on the coffins. Male and Dame? Mine and Daddy's? Murdered and Died? Matthew and Deborah? Meningitis and Diphtheria? Hock didn't fall asleep for quite a little spell.

He was wakened at dawn, remembering no dreams, by the touch of Mrs. Wilson's hand on his shoulder. When he opened his eyes, she said to him, "You really *did*, didn't you?" and as he rose up and began to harness the mules, she said admiringly, "I couldn't have done that to save my soul."

Not fully awake, he replied, "Wal, I reckon you knew 'em better than me," then realized that was not a decent thing to say.

"Yes," she said, expressionless, "I did."

The family served a fine breakfast to them, plenty of fried eggs with ham and grits, although the coffee wasn't any too good. Hock noticed that Mrs. Wilson wasn't eating very much and wondered if she was deliberately holding back so that she wouldn't vomit again from the rough ride ahead. She took Hock aside after breakfast and asked him how much she ought to pay these people for accommodating them. Hock explained to her that she shouldn't offer anything, that it might be considered an insult. So they both simply thanked the man and his wife and went on their way.

In the village of Fallsville, as they were passing the general mercantile store, where several people were sitting on the porch, Mrs. Wilson said, "Stop a moment," and at first, Hock was afraid that she was going to throw up again and right in front of those people. But she only wanted to go into the store. It was too early in the day for the store to be officially opened yet, but one of the men on the porch was the storekeeper, and he unlocked the store and let her in. She wasn't gone very long and returned carrying a bundle of what looked like wool cloth. She climbed up into the wagon and said, "Drive on." He did, but as soon as they were out of the village, she had him stop again. "Let's cover them," she said and showed him that what she had bought at the store was a pair of blankets. "I don't want people staring when we get to Stay More," she explained. He climbed down from the wagon and helped her spread the blankets over the coffins. The blankets didn't quite cover the coffins completely, but it was enough so that somebody sitting on a porch couldn't tell what the cargo was.

Driving on, Hock remarked to her, "Now, I'm not nosy, like you said, but I couldn't git to sleep last night tryin to figger out what the *D* and the *M* are for."

"They're just names," she said. "I'd tell you if I thought that you would drop me off in Stay More and go back home without meeting or speaking to anyone. But you might not."

"Might not which? Might not go home or might not meet or speak to somebody?"

"Either."

He did not challenge her or dig for more details. It was all peculiar enough already, he thought, without his making it any more peculiar; the less he knew, the better, he decided.

Something about Mrs. Wilson struck him as different, and studying on it, he realized that she had changed clothes. Yesterday, she had been wearing a satin dress; today, she was wearing knickers and a corduroy blouse. He'd never seen a woman wearing knickers before, but maybe that's what they do in the city, although the knickers looked as if she had put them on for the country, as if she planned to ride a horse or climb over a fence or something, except that she was still wearing the same fancy shoes she'd had on yesterday.

Feeling talkative this morning (they were getting to be like old friends now), he asked, "What all kind of shoe is them?" and pointed at her feet.

"Patent leather," she said, "with a bit of paisley at vamp, strap, and quarter."

"Vamp, strap, and quarter?" he said.

"This is the vamp," she explained, raising her foot and touching it, "and this is the strap, and this the quarter."

"I see," he said. "What's paisley?"

"The soft wool fabric with the pattern of swirls," she said. "I know that these shoes don't go very well with this outfit, but they're all I brought with me."

From time to time, Hock stole a sidelong glance at Mrs. Wilson and decided that she was not at all a bad looker. What he had mistaken yesterday for plumpness was not actually fat but just roundness: the shape of her face was round, and her short blond hair all covered by her close-fitting brimless hat made her look rounder than she was.

"What do you call that kind of hat?" he asked.

"It's clipped fur velour," she said. "I don't know that it has any special name."

"How come it's got no brim on it?" he wondered.

"That's just the fashion lately. Some ladies' hats have very small brims; others have none at all."

"It's a right pretty hat, anyhow," he said, but felt embarrassed and hoped she didn't think he was trying to get chummy. He shut up for a while.

But silence seemed unnatural this morning, as if, since they were getting to be fairly well acquainted, they had an obligation to continue chatting. She seemed to sense this too and asked him, "Why do your horses have the ends of their tails split?"

"They aint horses," he informed her. "They're mules. My dad split the end of their tails several years back."

"Why did he do that?"

"Aw, it's jist one of them old-time customs, 'sposed to cure 'em of something or other. They was bad sick, back then, though I disremember what with, 'cause I was jist a kid."

"Your mules are pretty old?" she said. "Do they have names?"

"Yeah, that'un's Ole Blue, and he's near 'bout as old as I am. That'un's Ole Gray, he aint but twelve or thirteen."

She didn't ask him anything else or say anything, so he felt it was his turn. He noticed that she seemed better adjusted to the rough ride of the wagon this morning. She wasn't making faces every time they hit a bump. He tried to think of something to say to her or ask her. Finally, a question crossed his mind, and he spoke it: "Is either of 'em a relative of yours?"

"Now, *that* is being nosy," she said. "But no, I'm not related to either." And then, as if to change the subject, she asked, "Did you go to school in Pettigrew?"

"Off and on," he answered.

"You didn't finish?"

"I finished, as far as it went," he said. "I can read good, and write fair, and do sums. That's enough."

She didn't seem to be able to ask him anything else, and he couldn't think of anything more to say. They reached the village of Swain before noon and turned northward into the Stay More Road. This passway was primitive, hardly more than a pair of wagon ruts that led through the forest. It was rough and hard on the wheels, by far the worst stretch of road they had met up with yet. She gripped the seat with both hands. Her purse fell to the floor with a thud. She began to look queasy again, and he stopped the wagon for a moment until she recovered. They were surrounded by woods of oak and hickory that seemed never to have been cut and to have been here since the days of the Indians.

He drove slowly for another mile, hit a bad bump, and suddenly, the left wheel slipped off and fell apart, and the back end tilted down, and the coffins would have slid off the wagon if Hock had not quickly jumped down and gone to stop them and hold up the corner of the wagon. He hollered to Mrs. Wilson, "Kin you git a fair size rock to prop under the axle?" He motioned with his head at one nearby. "That'un thar orter do it."

"Good heavens, you're *strong*," she declared, and rolled the rock under the axle, and Hock lowered the wagon onto it. "Oh dear," Mrs. Wilson said, looking at the disassembled wheel. "Now what do we do?"

"It was jist dry," Hock observed, "and the spokes come loose. Let's find a hole of water." Hock reassembled the spokes and wheel and slipped the iron tire back on, then, looking around and judging the landscape of the forest, went up the hillside and found a spring with a shallow pool of water beneath it. She followed him. He submerged the wheel in the water and weighted it down with a rock. "Have to leave it soak a little spell," Hock said and sat down on a fallen log. Mrs. Wilson sat there too, and even though she was farther away from him than when they sat together in the wagon, it seemed she was uncomfortably close.

"How far back was the nearest house?" she asked him.

"I aint seen a house since we left Swain," he said.

"And how far ahead is Stay More?" she wanted to know.

"Aw, it's hard to say. Maybe two mile or more."

"Then there's not anyone around?"

"I reckon not."

"All right," she said and suddenly reached into her purse and brought out a revolver. It was a small, lady's type of weapon with a short barrel. Hock hadn't seen one like it before. At the first sight of it, he was a good bit nervous, but she didn't point it at him. She closed one eye and squinted the other and took aim at . . . a tree, or nothing. "I want to learn how to use it," she declared. "I've never fired one before. Do you know anything about pistols?"

"Some," he said, "though I never seed that'ere kind afore."

She handed it to him. "Show me what to do," she said. "How do I make it work?"

Hock studied the pistol, located its safety, and flicked it on and off. "Is it loaded?" he asked.

Mrs. Wilson reached into her purse again and brought out a box of cartridges and handed them to him.

"Wal, let's see now," he said. "First, you put the bullets in from this side, here, one, two, three, four, five, six, like that, see? Then all you got to do is hold it like this and put one finger on the trigger and take your thumb and push down on the safety catch, then push down on the . . . the rooster. Now, don't forget to push back up on the safety when you're done usin it, or else you might shoot yoreself accidental."

A lizard was scurrying through the moss on the forest floor. Hock took aim and fired but narrowly missed. He snapped the safety back on and handed the revolver to Mrs. Wilson. She took careful aim at a tree and pulled the trigger, but nothing happened. She stared at Hock.

"You forgot the safety," he said.

Her thumb pushed the safety catch down, and she tried again. The gun fired. Its recoil wasn't very powerful but enough, along with the surprise of it, to topple Mrs. Wilson backward off the log she was sitting on.

"Goodness," she said. Hock helped her up. He couldn't help laughing a bit. But he reassured her, "After you git used to it, you allow for the recoil and keep your arm limber."

She tried again. And again, and was getting pretty good at it. But she was just firing aimlessly, at trees or at nothing that he could tell. She needed a target.

"What kinder game you aim to use that on?" he asked.

She looked at him for a long moment, not answering, and then asked, "What kind of game is it good for?"

"Purty small, I'd say. You caint kill a deer or a bar with it."

"But a man?" she said. "Or a woman? Would it kill one of them?"

"If it didn't, it'd make 'em powerful sick."

"All right," she said. She put it back into her purse, closed the purse, but then quickly drew it out again, wheeled, and fired at a tree behind her. She hit the tree. "If that tree were a man, would he have fallen?"

"More'n likely," Hock said. "But don't fergit now, like I tole ye, put that safety catch on ever time you let go of the gun. You coulda shot yoreself . . . or me."

"I'll remember," she said and snapped the safety on before returning the revolver to her purse. She lay the purse on the ground, took a step away from it, then snatched it up, whipped out the revolver, turned, and fired at another tree. This time she missed. She squeezed the trigger again, but nothing happened. She pulled the trigger several times in succession, but it wouldn't fire. She stared at Hock.

"It's empty," he said. "You've used up the first six bullets."

"That will be hard to remember, won't it?" she said. "I guess I'll have to keep close count."

She reloaded the revolver and went on "practising" until she had emptied it again and had hit four trees in succession.

"I reckon the wheel's ready now," Hock said and drew it out of the water.

"Do you think I'm ready too?" she asked.

"I reckon," he said. They returned to the wagon, Hock replaced the wheel, and they drove on towards Stay More.

CHAPTER 3

The road emerged from the woods at the crest of a long grade leading down into the valley of Stay More, and from this crest, they could see the whole village spread out below them, the farms of the valley, the hollows hemmed in by mountains. It wasn't a large village, but even so, Hock wondered what a village of that size was doing out here in the wilderness of Newton County. The valley was like a patchwork quilt of cleared land and forest land, the bottom lands along the creek planted with grain and several of the steeper slopes on the mountains cleared for pasture and vegetables. Yet even with all the cleared places, the whole valley still had a wild look about it, and Hock wondered if the people here would be the same breed of folks that he knew back home in Madison County. These mountains were taller; maybe the people were taller too.

"It's beautiful!" Mrs. Wilson said, and then she said or asked, "Why would anyone want to leave?" Hock didn't think that Stay More looked very much more beautiful than Pettigrew, but, come to think of it, he'd never thought about wanting to leave Pettigrew. "There's the school-house." She pointed to a distant white frame building with a bell tower on its front. "And that's the mill behind Ingledew's store." She directed his eyes toward a huge building covered with red sheet metal. "And up the road there toward Ledbetter Mountain is the bank, Swains Creek Bank and Trust Company." It was a small stone building at the end of the village's main road.

"You know the place, do ye?" Hock said, mildly surprised, for he'd somehow gotten the impression she'd never been here before.

"Yes," she said, pointing again at a house near to them. "That's the Duckworths'. And that must be the old Ingledew place. And up there beyond the blacksmith shop is Doc Swain's."

"Well, which'un you want me to drap ye off at?" The downgrade into the valley was steep; he had to use the brake and pull hard on it.

"First, we have to find a good safe place to leave them," she declared.

"Them?" he said, and, "Oh." Irreverently, he suggested, "How about the graveyard?"

"Not just yet," she said. "Look for a side road before we get into the village. I don't want to go through the village, even with the blankets over them." She pointed toward the stream of water coursing through the valley. "That's Swains Creek. There's a smaller stream, called Banty Creek, that flows into it from the east, and there are some caves or rock-shelters somewhere along Banty Creek."

"What if they aint any side road?" he said. "What if we have to go through town to git up Banty Creek?" They had already passed one house and been observed by the people sitting on the porch, who might wonder what large cargo they carried beneath the blankets.

"Oh dear," she said. "I think that was the Ingledews'. I hope those men weren't the Ingledews."

"Before, you said it was the Duckworths'."

"Did I? Well, that's right, I think. It *is* the Duckworths'. The Ingledew place would be the next one, and I hope we find a side road before we pass it."

They didn't, but there were no people on the porch of the Ingledew place, and not far beyond it, they did find another road branching off to the right, to the east, and Hock turned the wagon into it. This went only a short distance before merging with another and larger eastward road that followed a stream of water. "This must be Demijohn Road," she said. "And if it is, then that's Banty Creek." The road passed one house and then rose up through a rugged hollow into the woods. They traveled on, the area around them becoming more primitive, until Mrs. Wilson said, "There!" and pointed. A rock bluff loomed up behind the woods on the other side of the creek, and at the base of the bluff were several dark openings, caverns.

"Great sakes!" Hock exclaimed. "How're we gonna git 'em over there? I don't know as how we could even git 'em across the creek."

Mrs. Wilson looked disappointed. "Couldn't we at least try?"

Hock wanted to protest again that the graveyard was the proper place for them, but he said, "Yeah, I reckon" and drove on, looking for a place where the wagon could ford the creek. The creek banks were steep, and the stream itself looked too deep for the wagon. You're a fool, Hawk Tuttle, he said to himself, and then said to her, "What if somebody sees us tryin to git the coffins over there? Then you'd be in worse shape than if you never tried to hide 'em, wouldn't ye?"

Mrs. Wilson was almost in tears. "But what else can we do?"

"Damn 'f I know, really now," he said. "I don't know nothin." He began to wonder if the coffins would float. He realized he didn't have any experience in such matters, having never floated a coffin before or even, for that matter, watched somebody else doing it. Even assuming they would float in the first place, he, and probably she too, would have to get wet in the process, and then how would that look, if she, and probably he too, showed up at whatever place she was going to with wet clothes? You're worse than a fool, Hawk Tuttle, he said to himself.

He found one place where the slope of the creek bank was gentle enough to ride the wagon down, but as the mules entered the water, he saw at once that it would be too deep for the wagon. He halted the mules and yelled, "Back!" at them. They strained in the shafts to get the wagon back up the road. "I'm sorry, ma'am," he said, "but there don't seem to be no way to git over there."

"But couldn't you—" she began, then interrupted herself: "Look!" she said, pointing. "Why didn't I think of that before?" He looked in the direction she was pointing, on up the road, but saw nothing. "You can't see it from here," she said. "Drive on a way." He drove on, relieved to get out of the responsibility for getting the coffins across the creek. They rounded a bend in the road, came out of the woods, and there in a weed-grown clearing was an old log homestead, obviously not occupied. "The McArtor place," she said. "They moved out several years ago."

He drove the wagon into the yard, alongside the front porch, and said, "You aim to jist leave 'em here? If you worried about 'em spendin the night in that barn at Fallsville where I slept with 'em, how come you aint worried about leavin 'em here?"

"I don't think anybody would come here," she said. "And nobody would know they're here except you and me."

"Wal, you're the boss," he said and slid one of the coffins to the end of the wagon and lowered it to the porch and then kicked the front door open and dragged the coffin inside the cabin. The interior was musty, littered with rodent nests and droppings and whatever junk the McArtors had left behind. There was just one large room in the log cabin. He dragged the coffins up against the front wall, covered them again with blankets, then said to her, "I hope you aint aimin to leave 'em overnight."

"Why not?" she asked.

"It's terrible bad luck to leave a coffin all by itself the whole night long."

"That's your superstition, is it?" she said. "But I think they'll be safe here."

"Still and all, the rats might get into 'em."

"Oh?" she said. "Are there rats in there?"

"There's rats anywhere," he said.

"It won't be long, I hope."

He climbed back into the wagon. "Now where to?"

"The village," she said.

CHAPTER 4

The rambling two-story house, decorated with gingerbread woodwork, had a small sign hanging over the porch steps that said in faded letters, "Hotel." The building was unpainted, although it seemed to have been painted blue at one time. A number of chairs lined the porch, but nobody was sitting in any of them at the moment.

"Well, here we are," Mrs. Wilson said. "How much do I owe you?"

"Now jist a dadblamed minute," Hock said. "I aint very nosy, like you said, but if you think I aim to jist drap ye off here and go back to Pettigrew by myself, you got another think coming to ye."

She smiled. "I don't suppose I could make you leave."

"You shore couldn't."

"But there's really nothing else I need you for."

"How you gonna git back to Pettigrew? Or air ye?"

"I found you easily enough to bring me here. I can find somebody else to take me back."

"I aint in any hurry. How long you fixin to stay?"

"I don't know. If I knew, I might ask you to wait. But, you see, it might be one day, or it might be a week or more."

"You'd better git them coffins into the ground purty soon."

"*Shhh.*" She looked around, but there was nobody in earshot except a large hound dog staring at them from the porch. It seemed to be a well-mannered dog and had not barked at them.

"Could ye answer me jist one question?" he asked.

"I doubt it. But try."

"Do you know anybody in this town?"

"I know 'most all of them," she said. "Although I've never met any of them before."

He studied her answer and decided that it *was*, at least, an answer, so he decided to ask another one. "Do you have any notion of what you aim to do?"

"Yes," she said firmly, but then her jaw began to tremble. A shiver ran through her whole body.

"Maybe," Hock suggested gently, "jist maybe now, there might could be something else you could use me for."

She looked at him for a long moment. Then she climbed down from the wagon. She turned. "Driver," she said to him, "would you bring my suitcase?"

⚡ ⚡ ⚡

Hock had never stayed in a hotel before, if you could call it a hotel—only three rooms for guests upstairs but a room of his own, with a washstand and ironstone basin and pitcher filled with water, clean white sheets on the bed and white curtains on the windows, fresh paint on the walls and even pictures hanging on them, and the food was good and plentiful: for the first supper, they were served pork with baked beans, cornbread, good butter, cold buttermilk chilled in the springhouse, a platter of fresh-picked lettuce, radish, and onion. The woman who ran the place urged Hock to have a second and even a third helping, and he did. The table was large and round, and beside himself and Mrs. Wilson, there was a tall man named Willis Ingledew, who, Hock learned, was the village post-master and slept in the third of the three bedrooms upstairs and was the brother of the woman, Drussie Ingledew, who ran the hotel. Also at the table were three men and a woman who were nephews and a niece of the postmaster, although he learned the name of only one of them, Tull, from hearing the others address him by name. Tull Ingledew was taller than his uncle Willis, and better looking, but never said much. Hock meditated about the fact that everybody at the supper table, except himself and Mrs. Wilson, was an Ingledew. Ingledews all over the place. You could even afford to lose a couple of them, Hock thought.

In their talk at the table and afterwards, these people were politely curious without being nosy. Mrs. Wilson told them that she was a tour-ist from St. Louis and that she had hired Hock to drive her around the Ozarks. The Ingledews glanced at him as if for confirmation of this, and he nodded his head, although he was beginning to feel uneasy about her story and his part in it. Mrs. Wilson said she thought that Stay More was a very pretty village and, laughing, added, "I'd like to 'Stay More,' but I don't know just how long I can stay." When they learned that Hock was from Pettigrew, that brought forth a bunch of questions about various people in or around Pettigrew whom they knew or were distantly related to. Ozark people have first cousins and "last cousins" all over creation.

The last thing Mrs. Wilson said before going up to bed was to ask what time the bank opened tomorrow. Willis Ingledew told her that it opened bright and early.

Hock went to bed wondering if he might have become involved with a female bank robber. Maybe it wasn't even bodies in those coffins. Maybe it was gold. He began to feel nosy: he began to wish that she would at least give him a hint or two about what she was doing.

His bed was a very comfortable one, the mattress stuffed with down, and he was tired, but he couldn't sleep. He worried about the coffins being left alone. It is very bad luck to leave a coffin overnight. But *whose* bad luck? Not his; he was just her "driver," after all. But if she had bad luck for leaving the coffins overnight, her bad luck might be bad for him too. He lay in his bed brooding about that until he realized that he couldn't sleep. So he rose and dressed and sneaked out of the house, waking no one but the hound, who followed him as he walked up the Banty Creek Road. "Go home, dog," he said to it, but when he resumed walking, the dog followed him. "Suit yourself, then," he said to it, and went on, all the way to the McArtor place, where he found an old straw tick mattress, a sorry substitute for his feather bed in the hotel, but at least he might be able to fall asleep on it. The dog sniffed around the coffins and made a kind of whimper. "Dead people," Hock told the dog, then he lay down on the straw tick and said, "Good night, dog. You go on home if you want." But the dog lay at Hock's feet and went to sleep so effortlessly that Hock too drowsed right off.

When he woke at dawn, the dog was still there and followed him back to the hotel. He sneaked in the back door but could hear noises in the kitchen; somebody was already up. He went into the kitchen. It was Drussie Ingledew, starting breakfast.

"Up early?" she said. "You sleep good?"

"Real good," he said. "That is shore a mighty soft bed up there." He gestured with his thumb toward the upstairs.

"I stuffed it myself," she said. "With goose down." She pointed toward the kitchen window, and Hock looked into the kitchen yard and saw a great flock of chickens, geese, ducks, and guineas.

"What's your dog's name?" Hock asked.

"We call him Horace," Drussie said.

"He's a right nice dog," Hock declared.

"That old dog? He's smelly and covered with ticks. Sometimes I wish he'd just go off and find hisself a place to lay down and die." Then she asked him, "How do you like yore aigs fixed?"

"Any way," he said. "Turned over, generally."

He was finished with breakfast when the others came downstairs. Mrs. Wilson ate with Willis Ingledew and made small conversation with him.

Hock loafed on the porch with the dog, Horace. It looked to be a fine summer's day.

Mrs. Wilson didn't take him with her when she went to the Swains Creek Bank and Trust Company. The small stone building was just a short piece up the road from the hotel; there was no point hitching the wagon for that short a distance. She walked, and he went on loafing with Horace on the porch. The morning wore on, and Mrs. Wilson did not return. If she was robbing the bank, Hock thought, she was doing a real thorough job of it.

Across the road from the hotel was the main general store and post office combined, and Hock noticed that its porch, in contrast to the hotel porch, was filling up with loafers. He ambled over. Loafing, like drinking, is best done in company; the solitary loafer, like the solitary drinker, is liable to anxiety. "Howdy, boys," Hock addressed the men politely and sat himself on a nail keg. "Howdy, son," some of them said and resumed their whittling. Hock took out his Barlow pocketknife and idly whittled on a barrel stave. He was just as good a whittler as ere a one of them. The morning passed on. Willis Ingledew was writing a letter for an old woman who couldn't write. Hock listened in as she told Willis what she wanted to say to her son, who apparently had gone to California. Willis was a good postmaster, Hock decided, not just mailing letters for folks but writing them too. Willis finished the letter just as the mail wagon pulled up, and most of the men on the porch went inside to watch as Willis sorted the mail into the boxes. Most of the men got some mail, even if government pamphlets. Hock felt a twinge of homesickness, because his own mail was back at Pettigrew. Since he wasn't getting any mail here, he ought at least to *send* mail; he thought about writing a postcard to his mother. He took a penny out of the seventy-nine cents in pocket change, which was all the money he had on him, and bought a postcard. Willis Ingledew loaned him a pencil. He licked and chewed on the pencil for a few minutes and then wrote:

Deer Ma

Having rite peeculyar time over heer to Stay Moar. Jist thot to tell you in kase you git this afore I git back. Im fine, tho.

Yor son,
Hock

Then he mailed it in time to catch the mail wagon before it left. It was the first time in his twenty years that he had ever written to his mother.

A man wearing a suit and necktie, which was unusual for these parts, except on Sunday, came into the store and said, "Howdy, Willis. Anything for me?"

"Which lady?" the man said.

Willis handed some envelopes to the man. "Bank business and such," he said. Then he asked, "Meet the lady this morning?"

"Which lady?" the man said.

"They's a woman stayin over to Drussie's, said she aimed to go to the bank first thing this morning. Name of Wilson."

"Oh, *her*. Yeah." The man suddenly noticed Hock and began to stare at him. Like Willis Ingledew, the man was tall and lean, with a sharp-featured face; he reminded Hock of a schoolmaster he'd once had.

"That's her driver, she says," Willis Ingledew told the man. "Boy from over Pettigrew way, name's Hawk Tuttle."

"Howdy," the man said to Hock. "How long you been drivin her?"

"Jist a couple days," Hock said.

"Where are you taking her after here?" he wanted to know.

"She didn't say," Hock said.

The man turned to Willis and motioned with his head toward the rear of the store. "Let's look at the back room, Willis," he said, and the two men left Hock, who returned to the porch and resumed whittling. He was just as good a whittler as ere a one of these other men.

Noon came; Willis Ingledew closed the store and walked across the road to the hotel for dinner. Hock went with him. "Who was he?" Hock asked, casually.

"That was my brother John," Willis told him. "President of the bank."

"Sure are lots of Ingledews in this town," Hock observed.

"Always has been," Willis said.

Mrs. Wilson was at the dinner table. Hock was very happy to see that Drussie had fried a chicken for dinner. When Willis and Hock were seated, along with the three men and the woman who were nephews and nieces, Mrs. Wilson said, "I've been thinking about visiting Little Rock. Have any of you people been to Little Rock recently?" Now what is she saying that for? Hock wondered.

The various Ingledews seemed each to be waiting for another to answer. Finally, Willis Ingledew said, "Not that I know of."

Drussie Ingledew said, "But we've got two brothers live there."

Ingledews all over creation, Hock thought, but then he thought of something else. *Two* brothers.

Mrs. Wilson said, "Do you know of anyone in Stay More who has been to Little Rock recently? That I could ask questions of?"

Drussie said to Willis, "When was the last time John was down there?"

"Been two year or more, I reckon," Willis said.

"That's good enough," Mrs. Wilson said. "Where could I meet him?"

"You already did," Willis said. "This morning at the bank."

"Oh? *That* was John Ingledew?"

"Yep," Willis said. "That was him."

After dinner, Mrs. Wilson went back to the bank to ask John Ingledew what Little Rock was like, Willis returned to his store, and Hock asked Drussie if there was anything he could help her with.

"Why, bless your heart, boy!" she said. "I could shore use some extry firewood." She showed him where the woodpile was, and he took the axe and split up several armloads of firewood for her. The dog, Horace, watched him and retrieved any kindling that flew astray. After filling Drussie's woodbox, he pretended to loaf in the parlor and took from the fireplace mantel an old framed photograph of six young people and, showing it to Drussie, casually asked, "Is this you and yore brothers?"

"It is," she said. "Way back. That's me, and that's Perlina; she died young. And this is Willis, and here's John. These two here are the older boys, Denton and Monroe. They live in Little Rock now."

Denton and Monroe, Hock said to himself.

Then Drussie grew right chatty and commenced telling him the whole history of the Ingledew family, how Jacob and Noah Ingledew came from Tennessee in 1837, and one of Jacob's sons, Isaac, who had died only recently at the age of seventy-five, had fathered Denton and Monroe and John and Willis and Perlina and Drussie herself. "I was the least 'un," Drussie declared, "but I reckon that was a sight better than bein the oldest 'uns, which is what Denton and Monroe was, and bein the oldest boys, don't you know, they got the worst of it when times was hard, and Dad expected more of 'em. Even to his last days. I don't reckon Dent and Monroe would ever of gone down there to Little Rock if Dad hadn't passed on. It was like as if they was waitin fer him to go before they went . . ."

Well, Hock said to himself, maybe I don't hardly know anything else, but I think I know what *D* and *M* are for.

CHAPTER 5

Hock played checkers with Willis Ingledew at the store that afternoon and beat him.

"Purty good," Willis remarked. "Let's try it again." They moved the pieces back into position and started over. "How did you happen to meet up with that lady?" Willis asked.

"Wal, twice a week, I clean up the railroad station over at Pettigrew," Hock explained. "And she got off the train day before yesterday mornin and said she wanted somebody to drive her to Sta—to all these places like Stay More. I didn't have nothin better to do."

"She didn't say why she perticular wanted to see Stay More? I mean, comin all the way from St. Louis, you'd think folks up thar wouldn't never a heard of Stay More, let alone care to visit. We don't git many tourists hereabouts."

"Wal, she jist said it was the purtiest little place she'd ever seen . . ." Hock offered.

"Still and all, I caint figger what she's doin here. Been to the bank twice, but that's all she's doin here. Now she's talkin about goin to Little Rock. Hell fire, if she's so interested in purty little places like Stay More, why is she hankerin to visit the big town?"

"You got me," Hock said.

"Mighty strange," Willis went on. "John says she came inter the bank this mornin, and first she wanted to git change fer a twenty-dollar bill. Hell, *I* coulda done thet for her. But then she got right chatty with John and wanted to know what kinder stone the bank building was built of, and how long it'd been thar, and who'd built it, and all. You think she's right in the head?"

"Hard to say," Hock admitted. "Hard to say."

"Now she's gone back up there again," Willis observed, "to chew his ear about Little Rock. What does she want to ask him about Little Rock? If the water's fitten to drink? If they let hogs run in the streets?"

"Lord knows," said Hock.

"How much is she payin you fer drivin her around?" Willis asked.

"We aint discussed it yet," Hock said.

"And you don't have any idee how long she's stayin?"

"She tole me maybe a day, maybe a week. It depends."

"'Pends on what?"

"Wal, I reckon it 'pends on how long it takes her to git bored, maybe."

"Mighty odd," Willis said.

Hock beat him again, the second game of checkers, but Willis was pretty good himself, hard to beat, and there was nothing better to do, so they played a third game.

"Jist how many Ingledews are they in this town, anyway?" Hock wondered.

Willis counted on his fingers. "Wal, there's me, and John, and Drussie, and John's five boys and Lola; that makes nine, not countin Denton and Monroe, who went to Little Rock to live."

"What'd they leave for?" Hock asked.

"Money, I reckon," Willis said. "Figgered they could git a better-payin job a work down there. And they did too. But they been savin up, regular, and sendin their savins back home to John's bank, and I reckon soon's they git a few thousand ahead, they'll be a-comin on back home to stay."

"They aint married?" Hock asked.

"Naw. I aint neither. Us Ingledews has always been kinder shy about women. John's the only one ever got his nerve up, and that's 'cause Lizzie Dinsmore got it up fer 'im."

"So they live by theirselfs? Denton and Monroe, down to Little Rock?"

"Live together in one a those boarding houses," Willis answered.

Hock let Willis beat him in the third game.

⚡ ⚡ ⚡

Some of the younger men among the loafers on the store porch were talking about going up Banty Creek for a swim at a hole of water they called Ole Bottomless, and Hock was sort of hoping they might invite him to come along, but just then, Mrs. Wilson came walking down the road and came up to the store porch and spoke to Hock. "Driver, could we go for a little ride around the valley?" Without waiting for his answer, she turned and walked across the street to the hotel.

"High and mighty, aint she?" one of the loafers observed. "Don't she never call ye nothing but 'Driver'?"

"Wal, that's what I am," Hock observed, getting up from his nail keg. He went to the stable behind the hotel and hitched the mules to the wagon, then drove around to the front of the hotel and went in. Mrs. Wilson was having a conversation with Drussie Ingledew. Hock tried to eavesdrop but couldn't hear without being seen, so he waited politely out of earshot until she was finished, then said to her, "The wagon's ready, ma'am," and even gave her a little salute. He helped her into the wagon, then climbed up and asked her, "Which a ways? East? West? North—"

"Oh. That way, I guess," she said, and casually gestured north up the main road. This road, he noticed, as they drove up it, passed the stone bank building, and he noticed that she was taking a good look at it as they passed. He took a good look at it himself. It didn't have any sign out front or on the side either, but a building made from stone like that had to be a bank. Apparently, the stones were random pieces of sandstone taken from the creek bed when the water was low. The bank seemed to be just one large room in a rectangular box, with a small porch along the front, large storefront windows on the front, and two small windows on each side.

They drove a couple of miles up the valley and out of the village without Mrs. Wilson saying anything to him. She seemed to be lost in deep thought, and although he hated to intrude on the privacy of her thought, he couldn't help saying, "Any luck yet?"

"Don't," she warned him. "Please don't start asking me questions."

"Yes'm," he said. "Nice day, aint it?"

She looked around her at the landscape and sky, as if she hadn't noticed before. It *was* a nice day, very warm but with a nice breeze, the sky deep blue with white tufts of cloud gliding across it. Mrs. Wilson laughed and said, "I guess I'm not really behaving like a tourist, am I? Do you think they're fooled? Have you heard them say anything about me?"

"They think you're mighty strange," he informed her. "I reckon they suspicion there's a bug under the chip somewheres. Fr'instance, if you're so hipped on me drivin you to these small towns, how come you start thinkin about lightin out fer Little Rock?"

"Yes," she said. "I didn't play that card successfully. That was a ruse. I was trying to find out which of them has been to Little Rock recently. There must be *somebody* in that town who has been to Little Rock within the past week. That's the person I'm after."

"The one who killed Denton and Monroe?" he asked casually.

She gasped and nearly fell out of the wagon. He had to stop the mules. *"How did you know that?"* she demanded. "Who told you that? Where—" She closed her eyes and threw her head back and groaned, "Oh, God."

"There now," he said and patted her arm. "Easy. Nobody knows it but me and you."

"Then how did you find out? *I* didn't tell you."

"Like I tole ye, I've been right puzzled about them letters *D* and *M* on them coffins. So when Drussie Ingledew mentioned they had *two* brothers down to Little Rock, I sorta put two and two together and later asked her what their names were."

"I wish you wouldn't pry," Mrs. Wilson said angrily. "I wish you wouldn't speak to any of those people unless you have to."

"Wal, I did it casual-like," Hock protested. "There was this here photograph on the mantel, of the whole bunch of 'em when they was young, and I jist ast her what all their names was, and she called 'em all off, and there was those two amongst 'em."

Mrs. Wilson's anger went away, and she smiled at him. "You're pretty smart, Hawk," she said. "Drive on."

She didn't say anything more, so after a while, he remarked, "Right handsome lookin fellers they was too, when they was young. Did you know 'em well?"

"You aren't supposed to ask me any questions, I said," she replied.

"'Scuse me, again," he said.

"But I might as well answer that one," she gave in. "Yes, I knew them well. I was in love with them."

"*Both* of 'em?"

She nodded. A single tear came from her eye and rolled partway down her cheek. "It was pretty hard to separate them."

Hock was both puzzled and moved. He was puzzled by the idea of one woman being in love with two men, even if they were brothers, and he was moved by the idea of how a woman's love for two men would drive her to avenge their deaths. "Wal," he remarked, "it don't take no genius to figger out what you're doin here." She didn't comment on that. Another question occurred to Hock. "But tell me," he said. "What did *Mr.* Wilson think about all this?"

"My husband was killed in the war," she said. "I operated a boarding house. Denton and Monroe Ingledew were my boarders for the past three years."

"So you aint from St. Louis, after all," he said, "but Little Rock."

"That's right."

"The winderpane is wiped off a bit," he remarked. Then, since she'd answered so many questions already, he went on asking them. "Do you have any idee who might've done it?"

"That one I won't answer for you."

"Or why they done it?"

"That one neither."

"But you have to find out before you can bring the coffins into town and before letting the Ingledews know their brothers is dead? Is that it?"

She nodded.

"Wal," he went on, "is they any way that I could be any help to ye?"

"You're very accommodating, Hawk," she said, "but I—" She stopped, and a thought seemed to strike her. After a long moment of silence, she looked at him through narrowed eyes and asked, "Would you go so far as to help me break into a bank?"

Hock couldn't reply. That *was* going kind of far. That sort of thing was against the law. If you got caught at it, they would take you off and lock you up for several years. What he had in mind was helping her do some of her detective work, like poking around in the hotel attic or something, which, even if you were caught at it, they wouldn't lock you up for. But how could he say no after he'd been so generous in his offer to help?

"What for?" he asked. "How much you aim to steal?"

"I'm not going to steal anything," she said. "I just want to try to look at some records and documents."

"In the daylight?"

"No. We would have to get a lantern and go at night when everyone's asleep."

"I reckon they lock everything up, at the bank," he observed. "How are you going to get into the vault?"

"I think that what I'm looking for might not be kept in the vault."

"Still, you'd have to break open a door."

"Or maybe just get a window open. Do you think you could do that?"

"I might could do it. The question is, *Will* I do it? I aint none too eager to be took off and spend several years in a little room with iron bars in place of a door."

"All right," she said. "I guess I can do it by myself."

"Hold on, Miz Wilson. I aint never refused a lady a favor."

"Thank you," she said. "The name isn't Wilson. It's Cooper. But you can call me Emily."

CHAPTER 6

That night, Mrs. Wilson—or Mrs. Emily Cooper—went upstairs to her bed early, as appeared to be usual. It seemed she never stayed up much past eight thirty or so. Hock had agreed to wake her after midnight. She had told him she was a deep sleeper.

Hock sat on the front porch, enjoying the evening breezes. The dog, Horace, reclined on the porch floor near him, sometimes drowsing off and sometimes snapping awake to listen to the noises of the night. The air around the house was filled with lightning bugs, twinkling on and off in a steady pattern. Willis Ingledew and his sister, Drussie, came out and sat on the porch too and enjoyed the breeze and the lightning bugs for a while, then started talking.

"I shore caint figger it," Willis remarked. "First, she's talkin about lightin out fer Little Rock, and then, John says, she's talkin about settlin down in Stay More fer good. John says she ast him all sorts of questions about the bank, what all kind of services they offer, and whether or not she could store her valuables there, and so on and so forth. Mighty odd."

"Yeah," said Drussie, "and right after she come back from the bank, she started in to talkin to me again about Little Rock. Wanted to know if there was any way she could find out if anybody had been to Little Rock lately. Finally, I tole her you could put up a notice at the post office that if anybody had been to Little Rock lately, please git in touch with her over here."

"What do you make of it, Hawk?" Willis asked.

Hock scratched his head. "Maybe she's tetched," he said. "Best thing is probably jist humor her along. If she wants to find somebody who's been to Little Rock, then you'uns ought to help her find one."

"I aint heared of anybody hereabouts been to Little Rock lately," Willis said. "You'd think if anybody had been, they'd brag about it, and we'd of heared."

"Unless they didn't want anybody to know," observed Drussie. "Come to think on it, where did *you* go them three days last week, Willis?"

"I tole ye, I had to go up to Springfield, Missoura, to see about getting some parts fer the mill. What would I have gone to Little Rock fer?"

"To see the sights," Drussie suggested. "Or go tomcattin around with yore brothers." She laughed and winked at Hock.

"Pshaw!" Willis said, flushing. "John'd be the one to do that, not me. And come to think on it, where was *he* gone to last week?"

"He went up to Harrison to a bankers' meetin," Drussie said.

"So he said," Willis remarked. "But how do we know he didn't go larkin around down to Little Rock?"

"Lizzie wouldn't stand fer that," Drussie said.

"Which is prezactly the reason he wouldn't want anybody to know he went there."

"Wal, if that be so, he wouldn't tell that woman about it, would he? So how come she was talkin with him so much today? What all were they talkin about if it wasn't about Little Rock?"

"Yeah," Willis said. "Maybe they was talkin about Little Rock."

"Lizzie would be madder than a coon in a poke," Drussie said.

"It aint likely that woman would ever meet Liz and tell on ole John to her."

Just then, a figure came walking up out of the darkness of the road. It was John Ingledew, and he said, "Howdy" and sat on the porch with them. Speak of the devil, Hock thought.

"Why, howdy, John," Willis said. "We was jist talking about ye."

"Oh?" said John. "What about?"

"How was things down to Little Rock last week?" Willis asked him.

"What do you mean, 'How was things down to Little Rock last week?'" John said, with more anger than puzzlement, Hock noted. "How should I know? Whatever give ye the fool notion I was down there?"

"Jist speculatin," Willis replied, then he turned to Drussie and asked, "How long was he gone, Sis?"

"Oh, I reckon three, four days," she replied.

"So," said Willis. "Aint that a long time jist fer a bankers' meetin up to Harrison?"

"What business of yourn is it?" John demanded.

"Wal, me and Drussie have been speculatin maybe ye went to Little Rock."

"What would I go to Little Rock fer? Whatever give ye that idee?"

"You and that Wilson lady didn't talk about Little Rock?"

"So it's *her* put ye up to it, huh?" John said. "I declare, that woman is an exasperation to me." John Ingledew noticed Hock and said to him, "Now aint she, though? Don't she git under yore skin too?"

"Some," Hock said.

"Did she tell you we talked about Little Rock?" John asked him.

"She don't tell me nothin," Hock said.

Willis said to his brother, "Wal, did ye or didn't ye?"

"Shore we did," John admitted. "I was down to Little Rock two years ago, wasn't I? So I could answer some of her questions."

"What kinder questions?"

"Oh, Lord, I fergit what all she ast me," John said impatiently. "What kind of hotels do they have? Is there a theater? How's the weather in the summer? Do they have boarding houses? Stuff like that. She also said Drussie had told her we got two bothers living there, and she wanted to know if we heard from them regular, if they liked it and what all. I told her Dent and Monroe didn't write much, except to send deposits to the bank. That's what set her off on this other notion, about settlin down in Stay More and openin an account with us, and she talked about that fer a good little while."

"Right peculiar woman," Willis said.

"Real strange," Drussie said.

"Powerful odd," Hock said, and then he said, "Reckon I'd better hit the roost" and went up to bed.

He could hear the faint and distant sound of the Ingledews still talking on the front porch. He knew he would have to wait until they quit talking and went to bed before he could sneak out of the house and go keep company with the coffins again. But he got to thinking about that and how uncomfortable that old straw tick mattress was and how, if he was supposed to wake Emily Cooper at midnight and help her break into the bank, there wasn't much use in spending part of the night with the coffins anyhow and even if it was bad luck to leave them alone overnight, he'd already done his share, two nights in a row, and maybe after they broke into the bank, Emily Cooper would find what she was looking for, and then they could go ahead and bring the coffins into town and let folks give them a proper burial. What was she looking for? It seemed to him that maybe she suspected one of the Ingledews themselves, that she hoped to find proof that John Ingledew had done it, or Willis had done it, or even Drussie, or maybe all three of them together. Being a city woman, maybe she didn't realize that folks up in this part of the country would never kill one of their own folks, certainly not for money. Maybe a man might kill his brother for adultery, but not for money. Hock began to suspect that Emily Cooper was on a wild-goose chase. If only she would tell him what she was looking for or trying to prove, he might could be of some real help to her.

He nearly found himself drifting off to sleep but forced his way back and listened. The Ingledews were no longer talking on the front porch, and Willis's footsteps had come up the stairs and gone into Willis's room across the hall. But Hock decided not to go to the coffins. Even if he wanted to, it would be different now, since he knew who was in the coffins; it would be almost as if he could see them and knew who they were. Before, the last two nights, he hadn't known them; they were just bodies shut away in coffins, but now the bodies had faces on them.

The down mattress enfolded him snugly and tried to lull him into sleep, but he lay on his back, the best position for not falling asleep, and kept his eyes on the ceiling, imagining he was watching a square dance and evaluating the pretty girls there. This was good for an hour or so. Then he imagined a trip to Huntsville to see the rodeo, and this was good for another hour or so. He pulled his trousers off the bedpost and got out his pocketwatch and a match, striking the latter for a quick glance at the former. It was a little past midnight. He put on the trousers and the rest of his clothes, except for his shoes, which he carried in his hand.

On tiptoe, he went into Emily Cooper's room and located her bed and then her body and felt for her shoulder to give it a shake. He shook it gently and then again, less gently, and at length, Mrs. Cooper turned over and said "WHAT?" rather loudly.

"Sshh!" he whispered. "It's me, Hawk. Time to go out, if you still wanter."

The woman threw off the sheet that was covering her and got out of the bed. Hock turned away while she dressed, even though it was too dark to see much. There was enough light from the moon to see the woman when she was dressed; Hock could tell that she was wearing the knickers, and he realized at last what the knickers were for: for climbing through a window into a bank building. She sat to buckle the patent-leather-paisley shoes, but Hock whispered to her, "Not yet. Wait till we're out of the house."

Then they tiptoed out of her room and down the stairs. Even though they tiptoed as slowly as possible, one foot gently placed ahead of the other, the boards of the stairs were old and warped, and creaked. This sound made Hock sweat, and at the foot of the stairs, he paused for a long minute, listening to hear if anybody was stirred by the sound of the creaking.

They crossed through the parlor, where Hock paused to borrow a coal-oil lamp, and then went on out through the front door. The spring on the screen door also made a noise but a slight one. They sat on the porch steps to put on their shoes, then Hock went to his wagon and took from its toolbox a stove tool, a bench lifter, and a pair of wire pincers. A touch on his leg caused him to jump, but it was only the dog, Horace, sniffing around.

Horace followed them as they walked up the road toward the bank. "That's Horace," Hock told Emily Cooper. "He likes me." Hock noticed that Emily was bringing her purse and wondered what she needed it for, unless she really meant to steal something. Or maybe she just wanted to have her revolver handy.

In front of one of the houses they passed, a pack of dogs barked at them, but Horace answered them with a single bark, and they hushed. Still, all the noise made Hock pretty nervous, and he could tell that Emily was jittery too.

They came to the bank building and examined its windows. Without lighting the lamp, he began to probe with his tools around the bottom and sides of each window sash. But neither of the sashes would move. "Reckon they're locked from the inside," he said to Mrs. Cooper. "I'd have to bust a winder light to git at the locks."

"What about the doors?" she suggested.

"They're sure to be locked tight," he said.

"Let's try them anyway," she said.

They went up the front steps onto the porch, and he turned the knob on the door and rattled it, but it wouldn't budge. With his tools, he probed around the edges of the door without finding anything that would give. Then they went around to the side again and tried the rear door. He turned the knob and pushed, and the door opened right up! Mighty strange, he thought. Maybe John Ingledew was careless or else just didn't care. Nobody ever locked their houses or barns, but you would think they'd lock a bank. "Well, here you are," he said and held the door open for her and then followed her in. He put his tools down, closed the door, struck a match, and lit the lamp. It was all one room, except for one corner where a vault built of the same stone as the bank, and with an iron door, was cemented into the walls of the corner and another corner where a wire cage, like an overgrown chicken coop or dog kennel, with a locked wire door in it, ran from floor to ceiling, covering a roll-top desk and filing cabinet. The room was divided partway by the teller's counter, and behind this was another roll-top desk.

Hell, Hock thought, maybe they didn't even lock the vault. But the vault, he discovered, was shut tight. Anyway, Mrs. Cooper had said that what she was looking for wasn't in the vault. She told him to put the lamp on top of the desk behind the teller's counter, and when he did, she began pulling out drawers of the desk. He stood to one side, idly watching her, and then he found himself worrying about why the door had been left unlocked. Sure, it could've been pure carelessness, he realized, but also, somebody could've deliberately left it unlocked. But why? He wished Mrs. Cooper would hurry up, but apparently she had found something in a record book which was useful or interesting, for she was taking her time reading it.

Then she closed the book and replaced it and began on another drawer. Hock didn't want to seem nosy, but he wished she would tell him whether or not she was finding anything useful or interesting. She didn't say a word. Now she was taking a letter out of an envelope and reading it. Hock sort of moved closer and craned his neck and tried to see if he could read any of it over her shoulder, but he couldn't.

Emily Cooper finished with this desk and indicated the other one, closed off behind the wire cage. "Can we get into that?" she asked him.

He held up his wire pincers. "I'd have to cut a hole through it," he said.

"Go ahead, then," she said.

Although he was reluctant to do permanent damage, he took his wire pincers and applied them to one edge of the wire cage. But before he could cut one strand, suddenly the rear door crashed open, and a lantern came into the bank, followed by six men with rifles. "I jist knew it! Didn't I tell ye?" one of them said, and Hock recognized the voice as John Ingledew's. Well, Hock thought sadly, maybe they serve pretty good food down at the penitentiary. "Don't make a move," John Ingledew said, and then he turned to one of the others and said, "Tull, you ride up to Jasper and git the sheriff." Hock recognized the other men as John Ingledew's five sons.

"Wait," said Mrs. Cooper. "Let's leave the sheriff out of this, for the time being."

"What d'ye mean?" John Ingledew said. "We've caught you'uns red-handed, bang to the rights. I figgered ye might be up to somethin, lady, but I didn't allow as how the boy would be in on it with ye. Go on now, Tull, and fetch the sheriff."

"No," Mrs. Cooper said. "First you ought to read this." She took an envelope out of her purse and offered it to him. When she stuck her hand into her purse, Hock nearly had heart failure, for his first thought was that she was reaching for the revolver and was going to try to shoot it out with these men.

"Huh?" John Ingledew said, but he took the envelope. He gave the lantern to one of his sons and opened the envelope. There was a small key in it, along with a sheet of paper, which he read.

His face took on an expression of puzzlement and then astonishment as he read the paper. Hock noticed that the woman was watching his face closely.

When he had finished reading it, John Ingledew said, "Who's this here 'Emily Cooper'?"

"That's me," she said.

"Thought you said yore name was Wilson," he said.

"It isn't."

"But what does it mean here where he says 'if anything should happen to me or Dent'? Are you tellin me that something has happened to 'em?"

"Why don't you tell me?" she said.

"Heck fire, how should *I* know?" John Ingledew said. Hock figured that he sounded pretty innocent.

Apparently, Emily Cooper felt the same way. "All right," she said. "I suppose you don't really know anything about it. Last week, both of them, who were rooming at a boarding house which I operated in Little Rock, were found dead in their beds. The coroner said it was poison, but Little Rock police couldn't find a single clue."

All six of the Ingledew men had their jaws hanging open for a very long moment, and then, almost in unison, each of them said, "Naw!" If any one of them, or all of them, were guilty or innocent, then they were all equally guilty or innocent in their pretended or real surprise.

Then they began looking at each other and repeating, "Naw!" and saying, "It caint be!" and "Jesus Christ Almighty!" and other exclamations.

"How come we aint been notified?" John Ingledew demanded.

"I hoped to find the murderer first," Emily Cooper said, and then, her chin trembling, she declared, "I still intend to find the murderer, if it's the last thing I do."

"But what did you break into my bank for?" John Ingledew said.

"We didn't break in, we walked in," she declared. "You left the door unlocked."

"I did that a-purpose," he said. "I figgered if you was hankerin to git into my bank, no sense in havin ye bust somethin."

"How did you suspect I wanted into the bank?" she asked.

"Hell's fire, the way you was actin yesterday, all them questions and such. But come to think on it, you was jist tryin to find out if I was the murderer, wasn't ye? Yeah, *now* I see why you ast all them questions. What makes ye think I'd want to murder my own brothers?"

"For the same reason anyone might want to."

"And what would that be?"

"Their money," she said, and gestured toward the desk that she had been rifling. "I just discovered that they have nearly six thousand dollars in the bank."

"You got no business messing with the records," John Ingledew said.

"I am going to find the murderer," she declared.

John Ingledew looked at the key that was in the envelope she had given him. "I can match this and open their box," he said, "but there's not any money in their safe deposit box, I can tell ye."

"How do you know?" she said.

"Last time I looked, there wasn't nothing but some bonds and their wills."

"What were you doing, looking into their safe deposit box? You have no right to do that."

"I do too," John Ingledew said. "I got it down in writing, notarized by a lawyer up at Jasper. Dent and Monroe gave me permission to open their box to put in things they sent from Little Rock."

"Have you read their wills?" she asked.

"Naw, I aint got the right to do that. Have to get thet lawyer down from Jasper to open 'em. If you're sure they're dead. What proof have you got that they're dead?"

Emily Cooper reached into her purse again and took out another piece of paper and unfolded it and handed it to John Ingledew.

John Ingledew read the paper, reading some parts of it aloud: ". . . has permission of the State's attorney to transport said bodies to their final destination, as herein designated . . ." He finished reading it, and then he looked at Emily Cooper and just stared at her for a while, his eyes moistened. "Ma'am," he said, "we're obliged to ye. It is good of ye. Where are they?"

"At the old McArtor place," she said.

"Let's go, boys," John Ingledew said to his sons.

CHAPTER 7

Hock accompanied Emily Cooper back to the hotel, and then he offered the Ingledews the services of his wagon; it was the least he could do. They could go and get their own, they said, but it would take longer, so they might as well use his, and they thanked him and thanked him again for bringing the coffins all the way from the train station at Pettigrew.

"If she don't pay you, we will," John Ingledew said.

"I reckon she aims to pay," Hock allowed and harnessed his mules. John Ingledew climbed up to the wagon seat, and the other five men started to get into the back, but their father stopped them.

"Bevis and Tull kin come," he said. "The rest of you boys go on home and git the house fixed."

Hock drove the three of them up to the McArtor place, and they loaded the coffins into the wagon.

"What'd she want to leave 'em here for?" John Ingledew said. "Don't she know it's bad luck to leave a corpse by itself overnight?"

"Aw, I stayed with 'em myself last night and the night before," Hock declared. "I reckon she's really set on finding the murderer, and she wanted to keep 'em out of sight until she could find some clues."

"Has she found any?" John asked.

"Not that I know of," Hock said. "She don't talk much to me."

"How come *she* is all-fired interested in it? What business of hers is it who kilt 'em?"

"From what I kin make out," Hock declared, "she was right sweet on 'em. Tole me she was in love with 'em."

"Hhmm," John said. "Is she the one that they visited at the hospital one time?"

"She never said nothin to me about no hospital."

"Denton mentioned it in one of his letters. He never wrote much. But he mentioned there was this lady that him and Monroe went to visit when she was sick at the hospital. I reckon it was her."

"She aint tole me very much," Hock said. He drove the wagon, and John Ingledew directed him to the old Ingledew place. The four of them carried the coffins one by one into the parlor. Hock noticed the other

Ingledew boys had prepared the house: they had draped all the mirrors with white cloth and stopped all the clocks. It is terrible bad luck if you see yourself in a mirror in a house with a corpse in it. You'll likely die within a year. It's even worse luck if a clock stops while a coffin is in the house. Hock was relieved to see that the Ingledews were thoughtful people. John's wife, Lizzie, had been wakened and was crying and dabbing her eyes as the coffins were carried into the house.

They arranged four sawhorses in pairs, draped them with yards of black wool, and raised the coffins and set them upon the platforms.

"All right," John Ingledew said, "open 'em up." The son named Odell fetched a nail puller and began prying open the wooden lids on the coffins. Hock felt a vague sense of uneasiness, as if they oughtn't to be doing that without Emily Cooper's permission. But this was a foolish thought, he realized. The Ingledews had more rights to the bodies than Emily Cooper did.

The lids were removed and set aside. The Ingledews gathered around the coffins and looked down at the bodies. "It's them," John Ingledew said.

"Don't they look peaceful, though?" Lizzie said, and began wailing.

"Aint it a shame?" one of the sons said and turned away. Hock casually took the son's place among the gathering and looked at the bodies. They were almost identical, dressed in identical black suits with vests and neckties. Hock was a little shocked at the color of these men, or rather the lack of color; he'd never seen an embalmed corpse before. The one marked D—who was Denton—was a little bit larger than Monroe. Hock judged that both of them were close to fifty or over. Despite their lack of color, they were handsome men, with strong, chiseled features, and although, as Lizzie had remarked, they looked peaceful, they still had a determined look about them, as if they were just having a quick nap before getting back to work at a hard task. Hock found it hard to imagine that two such men could have been so shy and retiring as to never have married.

"Come daybust," John Ingledew said to his sons, "you boys git over to the cemetery and dig their graves. Me and Lizzie will set up with 'em." He addressed Hock, "Boy, you kin git ye some shut-eye. We're obliged to ye."

"Okay," Hock said. His pocketwatch read 3:00 a.m., and he was getting sleepy. He left the Ingledew house, but John followed him out onto the porch, clapped him on the shoulder, and said, "Son, did she ever say why she suspicioned that I might've been the murderer?"

"I tole ye," Hock said, "she don't talk much to me."

"Well, keep your ears open, jist the same."

"I am," Hock said. "Night."

"Night."

Hock got into his wagon and drove back to the hotel. Along the way, he felt a drop of wetness on the back of his hand. Turning his palm up, he determined that it was coming on to rain. That was a good sign. That made him feel pretty good, because it ought to always rain at a funeral. How did the old saying go? "Blessed are the dead that the rain falls on."

Hock said this aloud and drove on through the light drizzle to the hotel and went upstairs and slept.

CHAPTER 8

The whole town turned out for the funerals, even the preacher, who, Hock learned, wasn't needed, because neither of the brothers had ever attended church one time in their lives nor had ever been known to read the Bible, and they were, therefore, if not heathens, not Christians and not entitled to a preacher's service. But the whole town, including the preacher, turned out for the funerals, because all of them had known Denton and Monroe Ingledew. Hock estimated there were over two hundred people crowded into the small but pleasant cemetery on the north side of the small white clapboard church house. There was also a sizable number of dogs, including Horace. It was raining lightly, which was a good sign, and nobody seemed to mind getting wet, although Hock realized that the other people had an advantage that he didn't have: they could go home afterwards and change into dry clothes. He couldn't. During the brief service and the singing, Hock let his gaze wander over the crowd and wondered if one of these people might be the murderer. None of them looked like a murderer to him.

Emily Cooper had argued with John Ingledew before the funerals, trying to get him to postpone the funerals until she had more time to do her detective work and find out who had been to Little Rock, but the Ingledews didn't see any sense in that and thought it would be just as easy (or just as hard) to find out who had been to Little Rock after the funerals as before. It was important to get the dead brothers properly into the ground. So the whole town of over two hundred people came to stand around in the rain under hickory trees in the iron-fenced cemetery.

Even though it wasn't a Christian service, the preacher, a man whom they referred to as Brother Duncan, spoke briefly at the gravesides during the time that some of the women were dropping rose petals into the graves. He did not commend their souls to God but committed their bodies to the earth, saying the usual words about earth to earth and dust to dust. And then everybody (except Emily Cooper, who didn't know the words) sang a solemn hymn. Hock had sung this somber, mournful hymn at a number of funerals, so he joined in but noticed that Emily Cooper, who wasn't singing, was listening intently to the words:

Tempted and tried, we're oft made to wonder
Why it should be thus all the day long;
While there are others living about us,
Never molested, though in the wrong.

Farther along we'll know all about it,
Farther along we'll understand why;
Cheer up, my brother, live in the sunshine,
We'll understand it all by and by.

Hock realized that was a very appropriate song for this occasion, even though it was sung at nearly all funerals. Farther along, maybe, they'd know all about it: who had killed Denton and Monroe and why.

Then the younger Ingledew men began shoveling dirt into their uncles' graves, and Emily Cooper turned and walked away. She was nearly out of the cemetery before Hock could catch up with her.

"Wait," he said.

"Why?" she asked. There were tears streaming down her cheeks.

"You aint supposed to leave yet," he told her.

"Why not?" she wanted to know.

"It aint proper to leave until the last clod of dirt is in the grave."

"Oh," she said. "Is that your custom?"

He nodded and put his hand on her elbow to walk her back to the gravesides. The other people were looking at her, and some of them whispered back and forth among themselves. News travels fast in these mountains, Hock knew, and probably everybody here knew that Emily Cooper was here because she had run the boarding house in which the brothers had lived and that she was seeking to avenge their deaths. But how many of them knew why? he wondered. How many of them knew, or could guess, her attachment to Denton and Monroe Ingledew? Seeing her tears, maybe they could guess.

Finally, all of the dirt was filled into the graves, and then a strange thing happened: the Ingledew women and some of the other women of the village came up to Emily Cooper and hugged her and said consoling words to her, as if she were the widow of the deceased. She was clearly surprised but also touched, and her voice choked whenever she tried to thank each of them.

Then, before anyone left, John Ingledew raised his voice and said, "Could I have you folks's attention jist a minute, please?" Everyone turned their eyes to him, and he went on: "Maybe it aint proper to discuss this at a funeral, but I want all of you'uns to know, in case you aint heared yet, that my brothers there"—he gestured toward the two mounds of earth—"they didn't die; they was murdered. They was pizened. Now, I would shore hate to think that one of you good folks would e'er of done such a thing." He paused and looked slowly from face to face. "Who amongst you'uns would have a reason for it? What man would be so low as to—"

"You kin talk big at us like that, John," his brother Willis interrupted, "when how do we know you aint jist as guilty as ere a one a the rest of us?"

John Ingledew's face reddened, and he turned sharply on his brother. "Willis, that's a hell of a thing to say! Speak fer yourself. Would *you* of done it?"

"Haw!" Willis said. "No more than *you.*"

Did they really suspect each other? Hock wondered. Or was it simply that their grief kept them from thinking straight, kept them from realizing that a man would not kill his brother, at least not for the price of $3,000 per brother. That was a lot of money but much less than what a brother was worth.

The preacher, Brother Duncan, stepped between John and Willis and said, "I don't imagine this is the time or place for such a talk. We have committed their souls to sleep, if not rest, and we are beholden to depart this ground in peace."

One by one or in pairs and groups, the people left the cemetery and climbed into their wagons or onto their horses or simply walked back to their homes, until the only ones remaining, other than Hock and Emily Cooper, were the Ingledews. Willis extended his hand to John. "I'll fergive ye, John, if ye take back them words." But John Ingledew would not accept his hand, keeping his own deep in the pocket of his trousers.

"I aint fixin to shake hands with you," John said. "Not yet anyway." Then he turned on his heel and walked away, his wife and sons following him. His daughter alone remained. Her name was Lola; she was a girl about Hock's own age, but he didn't think she was much to look at. Still, if this weren't a time of bereavement, he wouldn't exactly disrelish the idea of setting his cap for her a time or two.

"Uncle Willis," she said, "I for one don't believe you'd ever do a thing like that."

"Thank you, Lola," he said. "I 'preciate it. Do you think yore dad would ever do a thing like that?"

"I doubt it," she said. "He was awful fond of Uncle Dent and Uncle Monroe."

"So was I," Willis said. "But I'll tell you what I'm gonna do right now, and I don't keer if you tell yore dad or not. Matter of fact, you might as well tell him. Tell him I'm gonna ride clean up to Harrison where they had that there bankers' meetin he was supposed to be at last week, and I'm gonna find out for a fact if he was really there all three or four days." Willis turned to his sister, Drussie, and said, "See you later."

"Aw, Willis," Drussie said. "It's coming up to rain pretty hard. Why don't you wait till tomorrow?"

"I don't keer," he said. "I aim to git this settled once and for all." He walked away and left the cemetery. Hock and Emily Cooper also left the cemetery, and a short time later, as they were walking back toward the village, Willis Ingledew on his horse approached them. "I'm off to Harrison," he said. "You plan to stick around till I git back?"

"Of course," Emily Cooper said.

"See you later, then," he said and rode on up the way.

"Maybe," Emily Cooper said to Hock as Willis's horse galloped out of sight, "if *he* is the guilty one, he isn't going to Harrison but instead making a getaway."

"Aw, I doubt it," Hock said. "If you ast me, aint none of them Ingledews guilty. Besides, he wouldn't leave without gettin the money first."

"Maybe he already has it," she said.

"Wal, what are you going to do then?"

"We'll just have to wait and see what happens," she said.

Hock wondered how long that would be. Uneasily, he also wondered if Emily Cooper was planning to cover his hotel bill. He couldn't very well come right out and ask her if she intended to. Well, he decided, if she didn't, he could just work it off, doing chores. Thinking of chores, he realized that his mother was probably getting restless at him for being gone from home so long. He decided he'd better send her another postcard and apologize. So when Emily Cooper returned to the hotel, he crossed the road to the post office, realizing at the last moment that if Willis, the postmaster, were gone to Harrison, the post office wouldn't be open. But it was. Willis's niece, Lola, was running it. "Howdy again," he said to her. "Need me a postcard." She gave it to him, and he gave her a penny, calculating that he was now down to seventy-six cents. His sweet tooth was acting up, so he looked into the candy counter and picked a marshmallow candy in the shape of a peanut. "Give me twenty cents' worth of them," he said to Lola, and she filled a small sack for him. That left him with fifty-six cents. He offered Lola a marshmallow peanut; she took one and thanked him. Then he asked to borrow a pencil and wrote his mother a postcard.

Deer Ma

Thay had thee fyunruls this morning, an I wint. 2 bruthers of Stay Moar. Thay still not fownd who done it, an I wood shore lak to fine out. So mite not git home today. Shore am sorrey not to milk thee cow and hawl warter an such, but will make it up whin I git home.

Yor son,
Hock

It was the longest letter he'd ever written, and he was tired when he finished. He mailed the postcard and offered Lola another marshmallow peanut. There was nobody else inside the store, only a few men loafing out on the porch. Lola didn't have anything to do but pretend to be busy, flicking a feather duster over the shelves and counters.

Her father, John Ingledew, came into the store. "Give me a can of Prince Albert," he said to her. She did, and he paid her for it.

Then she told him, "Dad, Uncle Willis has gone up to Harrison."

John Ingledew stared at her for a moment and said, "Oh?" Then he said, "Well, I've jist been thinkin about headin off for Springfield, Missoura, myself, to see if I caint find that there fact'ry where Willis claims he was gittin mill parts last week. You reckon he's got the address written down anywheres?"

"I'll look," Lola said, and she went to the rear of the store and disappeared into the small room that was the office.

While she was gone, John Ingledew said to Hock, "My own brother. Doing a thing like that."

"Which?" Hock said. "Killin 'em or accusin you of it?"

"Both," said John Ingledew. "He won't find no proof at Harrison. All them bankers at the meetin was from different towns. They wasn't any Harrison bankers there. He's wastin his time."

"Wal, what should he do?" Hock said. "'Sposin *I* was tryin to prove you was there. How could I do it?"

"You could ask at Pettibone's hotel," John said. "Ask 'em if I'd a had time to git to Little Rock."

"Does Willis know that's where ye stayed?"

"I doubt it."

"Why didn't ye tell him?"

"Hell, how'd I know he was going to Harrison?" John Ingledew protested. "But maybe I'll catch up with him on my way to Springfield."

Lola returned from the office, saying, "It must be one of these," and gave her father two slips of paper. He looked at them and then put them into his pocket.

"All right," he said. "I'm off to Springfield. See you later."

Hock asked, "You'll tell Willis about Pettibone's hotel if you should catch up with him?"

"If I meet up with him," John Ingledew said. He left the store.

"What's the Pettibone's hotel?" Lola asked Hock.

"That's where your dad said he stayed those four nights last week in Harrison." Then he asked her, "How fur is it to Springfield?"

"I never been there," Lola said. "But I reckon it's a right smart piece. Took Uncle Willis four days to get there and back in his wagon."

"Did he have anything in the wagon when he come back?"

"Uhm-hmn, he had a new wheat rolling machine and some spare parts for the corn roller."

"So he must a been to Springfield to git that," Hock observed.

"Or Little Rock," Lola said. "I reckon they've got mill parts down there too."

"You reckon anybody would mind if I went in the mill?" Hock asked.

"It's not open today, on account of the funerals," Lola said. "But as far as that goes, they don't never lock the door. Go on in, if you want. How come *you* are so interested in it?"

"I'm jist tryin to help that lady."

"She payin you for that?"

"I reckon not, but I aint got anything better to do, have I?"

Lola giggled. "You might could think of something better, if you put your mind to it."

He stared at her. Was she flirting with him? Well, he wouldn't mind, except it didn't seem proper in a time of bereavement to be fooling around. "I reckon I'll jist take a look at that mill," he said. "Try another marshmallow peanut," he offered and gave her one, then he went out and around behind the store where a path led to the mill.

CHAPTER 9

The mill was a sizable building—Hock counted four floors—of tim-ber-frame construction sheathed with red tin and roofed with tin. A broad-roofed porch ran the length of it, with steps leading up to this and a small sign, "Stay More Grist Co.," tacked to the front. The building was right on the edge of Swains Creek, but Hock, walking around behind to the creek, saw that there was no waterwheel and figured the creek water was used to make steam for the steam engine, which was housed in a separate shed. Hock went into the shed and studied the steam engine. It looked pretty old. He found the engraved metal nameplate covered with grime; he took a rag and wiped it off and saw that it had come from a foundry in Springfield, Missouri. Then he went up to the main door of the mill, tried it, and walked in. It took a moment for his eyes to adjust to the dimness of the interior; there were only two windows on the front. A crude and simple wooden staircase led to the second floor and then to the third; there was only a ladder from the third to the fourth. The whole interior was covered with machinery: grinders and rollers and hoppers. There was a mill at Pettigrew where Hock had taken corn many a time, but that mill handled only corn, while this one handled both wheat and oats as well as corn, and the milling of wheat and oats, Hock could see, was a much more complicated operation. He studied the machinery until he could determine which one was the wheat roller. It looked fairly new and had a clean metal tag on it that said, "Cornwall's Rolling Machine, patented 1889. B & L Manufacturing Company, Springfield, Missouri."

Hock inspected all of the machines in the mill and even climbed to the second and third floors and read whatever name tags he could find. Everything in the mill, every last thing, as far as he could tell, had come from Springfield. Well, he said to himself, it seems like Willis aint the guilty party. He was relieved at this proof, although he had never sus-pected Willis in the first place. Willis was too nice a feller to do a thing like that. Hock didn't believe John would have done it either, but if he had to pick one of the two, he'd rather pick John than Willis.

As he started back down the stairs, a man came into the mill and looked up at him and said, "Hit 'pears like we keep findin ye snoopin around in our buildings. First the bank and now the mill." Hock squinted in the dimness and recognized him as one of John Ingledew's sons, the one they called Tull.

"Why, I was jist studyin all this here fancy machinery," Hock said. "Yore sister, Lola, tole me the place wasn't locked, and I figgered to take a look. Right smart of fancy machinery."

"You aint 'sposed to be in here," Tull said.

"I never touched nothing," Hock said. "I was jist lookin."

"Find what you were lookin fer?" Tull asked.

"Yeah," Hock said, and decided he might as well not beat around the bush, because maybe Lola already told Tull what he was looking for. "All this here machinery was made in Springfield."

"Is that a fact?" Tull said.

Hock pointed. "It was that wheat roller there which Willis went to git last week."

Tull glanced at the wheat roller, then narrowed his eyes at Hock and asked, "Are ye sayin that means it must a been my dad who done it?"

"I aint sayin nothin," Hock said. "All I'm sayin is that Willis must of went to Springfield to git that there machine, so if he went *north* to Springfield, he more'n likely didn't go *south* to Little Rock."

"You're a regular brain, aint ye?"

"It don't take no brain. But there aint any sense in both a them rushin off to Harrison and Springfield when they could find out whatever they need to know without even leavin Stay More."

"What business a yourn is hit, anyhow, buster?"

"I'm jist tryin to be of some help."

"You jist might help yoreself into a power of trouble if ye aint keerful." Tull took Hock's upper arm in a powerful grip. "Come on. Git outen the mill." Tull led him out of the mill and banged the door shut behind them. "Why don't you jist go on back to wherever ye come from? Pettigrew, did ye say? Wal, if you're hankerin to snoop around, git on back to Pettigrew, and snoop amongst yore own folks." Tull's horse was tethered to a post on the porch; he untied the reins and climbed into the saddle. "I mean it," he said. "Fetch yore wagon and git out of town. Right now."

Hock sized him up. The man was about eight or nine years older than Hock and powerfully built. Hock wasn't afraid to fight him and knew that he could match him, if not lick him, but what good would that do? And there was some justice to the man's position: Hock really didn't have any right to be meddling in the affairs of people he wasn't even kin to. Hock felt an embarrassment, as if he had been caught and accused of terrible bad manners. He really had no business here. And yet he couldn't simply get out of town, just like that, without further ado. Also, he didn't like being *ordered* out of town. That, in its way, was terrible bad manners too. "You aint very hospitable," he said to Tull.

The man snorted a half laugh. "You're strainin our hospitality, boy. Now come on, I say, git movin."

Hock walked up the path back toward the hotel, Tull following on his horse. At the hotel, Hock said, "Wal, let me say good-bye to the lady."

"No need of that," Tull said. "Hitch your team and drive."

"Hell's bells, mister," Hock protested. "I never got paid fer drivin her over here."

"How much was she aimin to pay you?"

"We never discussed it."

"How much you want?"

"I aint thought about it."

"Think about it." Tull's voice was stern. Hock began to wonder why Tull was so eager to get him out of town. Did Tull know that his father was guilty? Or maybe Tull himself was the guilty party. Maybe Tull had been the favorite nephew of the two dead uncles, and maybe they had willed all of their money to him, and he had poisoned them to speed up his inheritance. But for all of his stern manner, he was a nice-looking feller, the best looking of these five brothers; he didn't look to Hock like somebody who would do a thing like that. Well, you never could tell. Looks don't mean much. Hock glanced up and down the road; there was nobody in sight, except the dog, Horace. Where was Emily Cooper? He sure hated to walk out on her without even saying good-bye. She would think he had become impatient or, worse, that he had become frightened and had funked out.

"I aint got all day," Tull said. "Name your price."

"Wal, it stands to reason the least I might expect would be ten or so."

Tull took a roll of bills from the pocket of his overalls and peeled off two fives and gave them to Hock.

"But what about my hotel bill?" Hock said. "I've done stayed two nights."

"I'll take keer of it," Tull said. "Hitch your team."

Hock shrugged his shoulders and led his mules out of the hotel's stable and hitched them to his wagon. Then he climbed up and took the reins. "Wal," he said to Tull, "I wish we could have been more friendly-like and neighborly. Stop in to see me if you're ever over Pettigrew way. Jist ask where Hawk Tuttle lives." He clucked at his mules, said, "So long" to Tull and then to the dog: "So long, Horace. Take keer a yoreself." He drove away.

Tull followed on his horse. "I reckon I'll escort ye a part of the way," he declared.

"Suit yoreself," Hock said. He sure is eager to see me gone, Hock said to himself. If he's not guilty or looking out for his dad, he sure must know something about something. Hock turned his head back and looked at the windows of the hotel, hoping to see Emily Cooper standing in one of them so that she could see that he wasn't leaving voluntarily. But there wasn't anybody in any of the windows. He turned his wagon into the Swain Road and began the long climb out of the valley. At the crest of the hill, he gave the village a last look and remarked to Tull, "That shore is a purty little town. I hate to leave."

"Yeah" was all Tull said.

Tull followed him all the way to Swain. So did Horace, until Tull snapped at him, "Git home, Horace," and the dog put his tail between his legs and slunked away. Hock was sorry to see him go. He and Horace had got along just fine. It was a shame that people couldn't get along with each other the way they could with dogs.

Hock figured that he and Tull might as well make conversation along the way, but Tull didn't seem to be very talkative.

"You know," Hock remarked, "come to think of it, I bet she might've given me fifteen, or even twenty."

"Yeah," Tull said. "She might've."

"I wonder," Hock said, "how she's gonna git back to Pettigrew when it's all over."

"She'll find a ride, I reckon," Tull said.

"You know," Hock remarked, "she really was sweet on your uncles. It's a powerful sad loss to her."

"To all of us," Tull said.

"Did you know 'em well?" Hock asked.

"Huh? They was my uncles, wasn't they? I grew up with 'em. Many's the time, when I was jist a spadger, they took me huntin or fishin with 'em. Many's the time."

"Seems to me like," Hock observed, "that whoever gits the money they left behind is dead certain to be the guilty party. And whoever that is—"

"Hush, boy," Tull told him. "You caucus my ear off."

He sure must know something about something, Hock decided. But what did it matter to Hock? As far as *he* was concerned, he might as well forget the whole business.

They came to Swain, and Hock turned his wagon westward onto the road that led over the mountains to Pettigrew. Tull stopped him and said, "This's as far as I aim to escort ye. You kin find the rest a the way by yoreself, I reckon."

"Yeah," Hock said.

"You know up from down, don't ye? You aint so dumb that you couldn't figger out what kind of welcome ye'd git if ever you come back to Stay More." Tull spoke these words as an actual threat.

"Yeah, I aint so dumb. Still and all, I caint help but think she might've given me fifteen. Or even twenty."

Tull took out his roll and peeled off another five. "Here," he said. "Drive on."

Hock took the bill and waved and said, "So long." He clucked to his mules and started rolling.

Tull sat on his horse, watching him drive away. Hock didn't mind that, but he hoped Tull was considerate enough to know that you aren't supposed to watch somebody disappear *completely* from sight, which is very bad luck and practically puts a curse upon the person who is leaving. Hock hoped Tull would turn away at the last instant, which any gentleman would do. And yes, sure enough, when Hock sensed that he was almost out of sight around a bend in the road, he looked back to see that Tull had turned his horse and was riding away. Hock appreciated it.

He found himself singing.

The time draws near, my dearest dear, when you and I must part.
But little you think of the pain and woe in my poor aching heart.
Good-bye, sweet girl, I hate to leave, I hate to say good-bye,
But I'll return to you again, unless I have to die.

This was an old song that Hock had learned from his great-grandfather when Hock was just a small boy, and he must have heard it sung or have sung it himself dozens of times, but he found himself wondering why he was singing it right at this moment. Well, he was singing to keep himself company, for one thing, and singing out of relief that Tull was a gentleman about turning away and not watching him ride out of sight. But that wasn't all. Thinking about the words of this particular song, he began to wonder if he really was so rash as to think about returning to Stay More.

He had his fifteen dollars, which wasn't at all a bad price for what little work he'd done, and his mother was probably getting impatient for him to come on home and get his chores done. His shirt and trousers were still a little bit damp from standing in the rain during the funerals, and if he drove the mules hard enough, he might be able to get home before tomorrow and put on some dry clothes or at least take off the damp ones and go to bed.

No, come to think of it, he wouldn't, because it had taken them almost all of two days to get to Stay More, and Old Blue and Old Gray were too old to be driven hard. He might make Red Star before dark, but then he would have to try to find somebody to invite him to stay the night. But it looked as if the sun might come out again, and that would partly dry him off.

"Whoa up," he said to his mules and stopped his wagon and just sat there for a while, trying to get his brains to working. *What if some harm came to her?* What if she discovered who the murderer was and pulled out her little revolver but lost the duel? What if, right this instant, she needed Hock to do something for her and couldn't find him and was feeling helpless and betrayed? By God, that would sure mortify him.

"Haw!" he said to the mules, turning them. "Back!" he said and backed up the wagon, then hawed the mules again and got the wagon turned around.

"*You aint so dumb that you couldn't figger out what kind of welcome ye'd git if ever you come back to Stay More,*" Tull Ingledew said to him again inside his head.

"I'm fairly dumb, I reckon," he said aloud. "I orter be bored fer the simples."

He had not driven far in return before stopping the wagon again, realizing he couldn't simply drive back into Stay More in broad daylight. Nor even, with his mules and wagon, in the night. And there was a chance Tull Ingledew might be lurking in the woods for a while to see if Hock dared to come back.

"Haw!" he said to the mules, turning them. "Back!" he said, and backed the wagon, hawing the mules again to turn the wagon around. One of the mules, Old Blue, turned his head and stared at Hock as if to wonder what was making him change his mind so often.

There was a place west of Swain—not a village, but a wide place in the road—called Edwards Junction, where another road led off to the north. Hock turned the wagon into this north road and drove on a way until he came to the first house, where a woman was hoeing her garden. He hailed her and asked, "Where's this road git to?"

"Boxley," she told him.

He drove on, keeping track of the approximate number of miles he was covering, until he had gone about the same number of miles as from Swain to Stay More and came to another little hamlet no more than a wide place in the road and, stopping at a house there, learned that it was called Sidehill, an appropriate name because this less than a town was located on the side of a hill. A rough trail ran eastward up the hill, and Hock guessed that it led to Stay More.

Hock said to the farmer, "I was on my way up to Boxley, but these here mules is all tuckered out and won't make it. Do you reckon I could leave 'em with you while I go the rest of the way on foot?"

"Shore," the man said. "Let 'em go in the back pasture yonder."

Hock unhitched his wagon and led the mules through a gate and removed their harness, turning them loose in the fenced pasture. When he returned to the house, the man said, "Come eat you some supper with us."

"I thank ye kindly," Hock said, "but I reckon I best git on."

"No sense in that," the man said. "Fill yore belly afore ye light out."

"I wouldn't put you'uns to any bother," Hock said.

"No bother atall, boy," the man said.

"I'm obliged and beholden," Hock said, and stayed to eat supper with the family, which consisted of the man and his wife and four children. The woman served chicken and dumplings with plenty of good cold buttermilk from her springhouse.

"Who you visitin at Boxley?" the man asked Hock after they had eaten.

"Aw, I aint visitin anybody particular," Hock said, trying to think of some excuse. "I was jist goin to a store up there," he said, hoping that Boxley had one.

"You mean Villines' store?" the man asked.

"Yeah, that's the one," Hock said. "I was aimin to see Villines about some stuff."

"Reckon he'll be closed up, time you git thar on foot," the man said. "Better jist stay the night with us."

"Thank ye, but I guess I'll git on."

"Don't rush off," the man invited. "We kin put ye up easy."

"I 'preciate it a heap," Hock said, "but I believe I'll go on to Boxley."

"It's all of seven mile and mostly uphill, and Villines is shore to be closed. Stay the night with us."

That was the man's third offer, and Hock knew that to decline an offer thrice is final. He thought, briefly, about staying here and sneaking off after bedtime, but that would look suspicious, especially if he left his mules in the pasture. "I shore thank ye kindly," Hock said, "but I'd like to git on."

"Shore," the man said. "Leave yore mules long as ye like."

Hock thanked the man again, thanked the woman for the supper, and walked on up the road toward Boxley. Out of sight of the house, he left the road and went eastward through the woods, up the hill and over it, where he regained the rough passway that he supposed led to Stay More. It was still full daylight, and the sun hadn't dropped yet, but he figured it would be getting dark by the time he reached Stay More. He hoped there wouldn't be any houses along this trail; if there were, he would have to circle through the woods behind them. He didn't want to be seen.

But there were houses on this trail. Rounding a hill, he heard dogs barking in the distance and knew he was approaching a house. He cut to his left through the woods and made his way down the hill behind the house. The dogs kept barking, and one of them found Hock and bayed at him. "Hush, dog," Hock said and walked rapidly on, but the dog followed him, baying, for half a mile through the woods, until he was beyond the house and could regain the trail. It occurred to Hock that he had been to a lot of trouble already and was going to a lot more trouble, meddling in something that wasn't rightly any of his business in the first place. But it also occurred to Hock, perhaps for the first time, that he was awfully fond of Emily Cooper and would do anything in the world for her. He smiled and went on.

CHAPTER 10

If he hadn't become lost, Hock would have arrived in Stay More too early, while folks were still up and about. As it was, he went north of the Low Gap Road for three miles before discovering that it was the wrong road, and by the time he had corrected the error, retracing his steps to the trail that led from Sidehill to Stay More, it was past most everyone's bedtime, and when he finally found Stay More sleeping in the moonlight, there was not a light anywhere in the village.

He went straight to the hotel, where he was accosted by the dog, Horace, who quietened when Hock spoke softly to him and gave him his hand to sniff. A dog, if he knew you, wouldn't mind having you around, no matter what his masters thought of you. Hock gave Horace a few head pats, then he went around to the back door of the hotel and took off his shoes. He opened the screen door slowly to keep the spring from creaking, but still it slightly creaked.

He gentled the door open and closed it slowly behind him, then tiptoed slowly to the stairs and up them, placing his feet carefully on each step so the boards wouldn't rasp. It seemed to take him a long time, but he was in no hurry. He went into Emily Cooper's room and closed the door behind him. He stooped over her bed and found her shoulder and gave it a gentle shake and then another shake, less gentle.

She came awake with a start. "WHAT?"

"Sshh, it's me, Hawk," he said.

"HAWK?"

"SSshh!" he said.

She lowered her voice and sat up in the bed. "Hawk? Where have you been?"

"I got run out of town," he whispered.

"How? Who? Where . . . ?" She patted the bed. "Here. Sit down."

He sat on the edge of the bed and told her everything that had transpired between him and Tull Ingledew.

"I had a feeling Tull should be a suspect too," Emily Cooper said.

"I don't know about that," Hock said, "but I know it weren't Willis. What I was doin in the mill when Tull caught me was I was lookin at that machinery. All of it come from Springfield, Missoura. So Willis must've been there last week."

"And Willis returned from Harrison late this evening saying he found a man there who would be willing to testify that John was in Harrison all of those four days last week. So it seems that neither John nor Willis is guilty, unless—"

"I tole ye," Hock interrupted. "I tole ye a man wouldn't murder his own brothers, leastways not for no money like three thousand or even six thousand."

"Unless," she continued, "one or the other or both of them had somebody else do it for them. Like Tull. If Tull wanted you out of town, he must have been afraid that you would eventually stumble upon a secret." She patted his hand and said, "I'm so glad you came back, Hawk! If you hadn't, I wouldn't have known to suspect Tull. Now I've got to find out if he was gone from Stay More last week."

"If you let on to Tull how you suspicioned him, he'll know I'm back in town."

"I won't let on," she said. "But you'll have to keep out of sight, won't you?"

"Yeah, I reckon I'd better lay low."

"Where?"

"The old McArtor place, maybe," he told her. "If it hid the coffins, it can hide me."

"But what will you sleep on? There aren't any beds in that cabin, are there?"

"There's an old straw tick mattress," he told her, without telling her that he had already slept on it one night.

"What will you do for food?"

"I'll manage."

"Let me bring you something tomorrow."

"No need to do that. You'll be busy, I hope."

"Not too busy to bring you something to eat."

It was, in a sense, her third invitation, so he could not decline. "Wal, thanks. I 'preciate it." He stood up and said, "You take keer tomorrow. Hear?"

"I will," she said. She rose from the bed and opened a chest of drawers and took out a blanket and gave it to him. "You might need this," she said.

Before he could get away, she kissed him on his cheek.

※※※

Horace followed him to the old McArtor place. He let the dog into the cabin, saying to him, "It'd be right lonesome up here without ye." Hock lay on the old straw tick mattress and covered himself with the blanket, glad that Emily Cooper had given it to him, because it might get a bit chilly before dawn. Horace curled at his feet and went right to sleep. The dog didn't smell too good, but neither did the interior of the old cabin, and Hock didn't have time to think about either of them before he fell asleep.

The sun was well up in the sky when he woke, remembering no dreams but troubled with a sense of helplessness and restlessness. He had slept too late, but what difference did it make? He didn't have anything to do. He went out behind the cabin to the well. The rope was rotten, and the bucket was rusted and full of holes, but he managed to draw up enough water to slake his thirst and splash his face, then he found a cracked bowl and poured some water for Horace. The dog drank noisily. "Sorry there's nothin to eat," he said to Horace. He wished he were in Pettigrew, faced with the plate his mother would set out for him: six fried eggs, fresh-baked biscuits with sorghum molasses, and her homemade pork sausage, with lots of coffee. Thinking of this made his stomach growl so loudly that Horace gave him a questioning look.

"Horace, you might as well go on home and git you somethin to eat," he said to the dog, but the dog didn't move. "Bring me a leftover biscuit if you find one," he said, and Horace looked at him as if he was sorry that he couldn't understand what Hock was saying. Hock motioned with his arm. "Go on home, Horace," he said gently, and the dog turned and started back toward the village.

Hock went into the cabin. In the daylight, he saw again how filthy the place was and realized he must have been awfully tired those two nights to have been able to sleep on such a poor mattress among such dirt and decay. He didn't think he would be able to do it another night, and he hoped that Emily Cooper was having a lot of luck finding the murderer.

Around noon, he hoped that Emily Cooper wasn't having so much luck finding the murderer that she would forget to bring him something to eat.

The afternoon wore on and was hot. He wanted to walk over to Banty Creek and find that swimming hole they called Ole Bottomless, but he couldn't take the chance of being seen.

At suppertime, he was about ready to give up hope of seeing Emily Cooper. But he decided she might be waiting for the cover of darkness to come to the cabin.

He waited until well past dark, sitting out on the porch now without fear of being seen, and still she did not show up. He began to play a little game in his mind. *I will count to twenty, then she will appear in the road.* He counted to twenty several times. Then he changed the game to counting to a hundred. He tried that several times too, but it didn't work.

When bedtime came, he began walking back toward the village. The hotel was dark. Horace didn't bark at him this time, because he knew him well enough by now. Hock crept upstairs to Emily Cooper's room and groped to find her shoulder, but there was no shoulder to find.

⚡ ⚡ ⚡

He sat down on the bed and waited. Maybe she just had to go out back for a few minutes and would return. Hock, sitting there, thought about tiptoeing down to the kitchen to see if he could find a bite of anything to eat. But he was reluctant to risk being heard fumbling around in the dark. And he wanted to be sure to be here if Emily Cooper came back.

But she didn't. He didn't know how long he waited, but she didn't come back. Had she left for good? He struck a match and held it aloft and could just make out, against the wall, the shape of her suitcase. So she had not left. But where was she? Hock was very patient, but he began to realize that it wasn't doing anybody any good for him to keep sitting there.

He got up and left the house the way he had entered, through the back door. Horace was still awake, wagging his tail in the moonlight as Hock approached. "Seen the lady, Horace?" Hock whispered to the dog and thought, *I keep on talking to this old dog as if he could understand me, but I reckon that's jist as good as talking to myself.* "Whichaway did the lady go, Horace?" he said. The dog wagged his tail but did not reply. Then, as Hock was talking to the dog, he noticed an object on the ground nearby. He bent to pick it up and hold it to the moonlight. It was a patent leather shoe with a bit of paisley at vamp, strap, and quarter. Hock remembered Emily Cooper explaining which was the vamp and the strap and the quarter. One shoe. He searched around but couldn't find the other one. What would she have dropped one shoe for? he wondered. *Maybe it's a message for me,* he decided. Maybe she's trying to tell me that this is where they got her, and if I could just find the other shoe, that's where they took her.

But who was "they"? Or *him*? Where did Tull Ingledew live? As far as Hock had been able to figure it, Tull and his unmarried brothers still lived at John's house, the big old Ingledew place, just as Hock himself still lived with his folks. Thinking of this, he wished for a moment that he was home in his bed instead of out hunting for a lady's shoe.

"Where's the other shoe, Horace?" he said to the dog, but the dog just wagged his tail. Hock walked on to the Ingledew house, and Horace tagged along beside him. The Ingledews had a pack of dogs that ran out and started to make a fuss, but Horace spoke to them, and they shut up. Quickly, Hock searched the ground around the gate and went through it, searching the front yard, but found no shoe. This intrusion became too much for the Ingledews' dogs, who resumed barking at him despite Horace. A lantern was lit within the house, and Hock retreated quickly, going back down the road into the village.

Maybe Tull Ingledew didn't live there, he thought. Or maybe, if Tull did live there, that's not where he took her. Or maybe he wasn't the one who took her. Or maybe the shoe didn't have anything to do with it anyhow. But what else could Hock do? He went on looking for the shoe. He looked around the schoolhouse and the store and post office, then around the mill. The moon was going to set soon, he noticed, and then he'd have to wait for daybust to keep on looking, or else steal a lantern.

Horace was still following him. "Where on earth is the other shoe, Horace?" he said. He thrust the one shoe under Horace's nose. "Take a good sniff," he said. "Now trail, Horace, *trail!*" Hock was pleased to see that Horace began sniffing around on the ground. Maybe he wasn't so dumb after all. Horace moved in a zigzag direction, sniffing randomly and aimlessly at the ground, and Hock followed him. Once back on the main road, Horace's direction straightened out: he seemed to pick up a scent and moved more rapidly up the main road of the village. Hock hoped that he knew what he was doing. As they passed other houses on the road, other dogs barked at them, but they passed rapidly on until they were at the north end of the village, where the bank was.

Horace stopped at the bank. After sniffing around the front porch of the bank, he trotted around to the rear door, and there, beside the wooden steps leading up to the door, the same door he and Emily Cooper had entered two nights before, Horace found a patent leather shoe with a bit of paisley at vamp, et cetera, and picked it up in his mouth and presented it to Hock, wagging his tail mightily. "Good dog," Hock said to him. He figured "they" must have locked her up in the bank, if not in the vault, then behind that wire cage. He rattled the doorknob and found that it was locked this time. He put his mouth to the crack of the door and said

"EMILY?" as loud as he dared. There was no answer. He tried looking through the windows, but it was too dark in there to see anything.

Again, he put his mouth to the door and said "EMILY?" almost but not quite loud enough to wake the village.

He waited, listening. Maybe they gagged her, he thought. But then a human voice made a noise that sounded to him like "Hawk?"

"Emily?" he said. "Are you in there?"

The voice said something that sounded like "Yes."

"Hang on," he said. "I'm a-comin in." Not caring about anything this time except getting her out, he took a rock and busted a windowpane and reached his arm through and found the window catch and opened it, then pushed up the sash and climbed through the window. He went straight to the wire cage and said, "Are you all right?"

"Yes," she said. "You're wonderful, Hock."

"You left them shoes for me, didn't ye?"

"Yes," she said. "I hoped you would find them."

"Wal, I found one of 'em. Horace found the other'n."

"Who's Horace?"

"My dog. I mean, he's Drussie Ingledew's dog, but he's been followin me around a lot lately." Hock rattled the door of the wire cage. "How'm I gonna git this durn thing open?"

"Where are your wire pincers?"

"Left 'em in my wagon, miles west of here," he told her and then asked, "Who put ye in here? Was it Tull?"

"No, his father. He says he's just holding me here temporarily. They're bringing the sheriff from Jasper tomorrow."

"How come?"

"They think that *I* poisoned Denton and Monroe."

Hock thought about that. The thought had slipped through his head a couple of times before, but he had dismissed it. Emily Cooper was too nice a lady to do something like that. "You never," he said. "Did ye?"

"Of course not," she said. "But John Ingledew came back from Springfield satisfied that Willis had been up there all the time he was gone last week. And Willis was already back from Harrison, satisfied that John had been there. And Tull, it turns out, was only interested in protecting his father. That's why he ran you out of town. I suppose you could take it as a compliment that Tull thought you were too smart. Tull wasn't any-where last week; I mean, Drussie swears that he was here in Stay More all of last week. So this afternoon, John fetched a lawyer down from Jasper, and I gave him the key I had from the brothers for their safe deposit box, and they opened it and took out the wills, and the lawyer read them." She stopped.

"Yeah?" Hock said. "Go on."

"Except for leaving a hundred dollars each to their niece and five nephews"—Emily's voice choked, and Hock could tell that she was softly weeping—"except for that, they left everything to *me*."

Hock studied it. Was Emily Cooper really too nice a lady to poison a couple of old bachelors to get their money? Maybe, he wondered, she was just shrewd. Maybe this whole business of being so dead set on finding their murderer was just her game to cover up her own tracks. Yet still and all, it was right painful to think of Emily Cooper as a murderer.

"You know, from what I've heard," he remarked, "pizenin is gener'ly done by a woman, not a man. Is there any way that you could prove you didn't do it?"

"The Little Rock police considered me a suspect for a while," she declared, "and they questioned me at length but satisfied themselves that I wouldn't have done it. They searched my house thoroughly without finding any poison, and they checked and tested the leftover food, and they . . ." Her voice broke again. "I *loved* them, Hawk! I don't want their money! I just want to find their murderer and kill him!"

"But if John didn't do it, and Willis didn't do it, and Tull didn't do it, who did?"

"As you say, poisoning is a woman's way of murder. And the only suspect I can think of is Drussie. When the wills were read, none of the Ingledews except Drussie expressed very much personal disappointment, only surprise that the money was left to me. But Drussie, I think, was disappointed. She complained loudly. She seemed to act as if she had expected a large share. I'm very suspicious of her. I want to find out if there was any possibility she was gone from Stay More last week."

"How do ye aim to do that?" he asked. "First it was me that wasn't welcome around here. And now it looks like you aint welcome neither. If aint neither one of us able to do nothing, how are we gonna keep on lookin fer the murderer?"

"Can you get me out, Hock?" she asked. "Or not?"

"Let me think a minute," he said, and he studied it, but for more than just a minute. It was complicated. If she was guilty, then he would be helping her escape. If she was innocent, he couldn't see what good it would do for her to be let out anyhow. How, in the first place, could he get her out? He'd have to have some wire cutters, but even if he had his pair of pincers right now in his hand, he didn't know if he would, or could, use them. A thought occurred to him: How did she happen to have her shoes in her hand to drop as a trail for him to follow? Either she was sneaking out of the hotel when she was caught—sneaking with her shoes in her hand—or else she deliberately planned to leave the trail of shoes for him to follow as her only way of getting his help. Either way, it looked as if she might be guilty.

When he went on thinking and said nothing more, she said, "Well, I suppose you don't believe me either. In that case, why don't you go on home? You've wasted enough time here already."

"Naw," he said. "I don't reckon I'll quit jist yet. Answer me a question: How come ye to have yore shoes in yore hand when ye left the hotel?"

"I didn't leave it. I was taken from it. By John Ingledew. I had hoped to bring you some food, but I couldn't leave the house without being seen by the Ingledews, so I pretended to go up to bed and wait until the Ingledews had gone to bed to bring you your supper. But they stayed up a long time, talking; apparently, that was when they decided to suspect me. So John Ingledew came up and got me and said he intended to lock me in this bank and go to Jasper for the sheriff tomorrow—today—it's well past midnight, isn't it? Anyway, I didn't put on my shoes. I dropped them, one there, one here. It was my only hope you'd find me."

"That was a bright idee," he admitted.

"Not as bright as your finding me," she said.

"Shucks," he protested. "It weren't nothing. And Horace helped."

"Please get me out," she said.

There was one more question he had to ask. "Do ye have the money yet?"

"I told you, I don't want it."

"That aint the same as not having it. Do ye or not?"

"Yes, I have it. John Ingledew was required by law in the presence of the lawyer who read the wills to make out a check for the amount and hand it to me. It is in my purse. Since it has my name on it, I couldn't very well return it, could I?"

Well, that just about settles it, Hock decided. He didn't think he could let her out now. She was just fooling around with him, maybe. If he let her out, he would be a—what do you call them?—he would be an "accomplice," and if he was caught, he'd go to jail with her. Still, it sure did pain him to think that such a nice lady would have done such a thing.

Hock squatted, sitting on his heels, country fashion, like a stumped hunter meditating on a broken rifle. Where would he find wire cutters even if he did want to get her out? If he went to get his own out of the wagon, it would take him till after daylight to get there and back.

"What are you doing?" she asked.

"I'm jist a-settin here," he told her.

"Can you see me?" she asked.

"Some," he said. The moon had set, but there was yet enough pale light from the night sky coming through the large front windows of the bank so that he could make out her form sitting at the desk behind the wire cage.

"Can you see what I've got in my hand?" she asked.

He squinted. No, he couldn't tell what she was holding. "Naw," he said.

"I have my revolver, Hawk," she said, "and it's pointed at you. If you won't get me out of here, I'll shoot you."

Hock swore. Then he said, "Now, that's mighty dumb, lady. It shore is. That is the dumbest thing ever I heared."

"But I mean it," she said, though her voice trembled.

"Naw," he said. "You jist think about it. Think about how I'd have to leave here anyway to git something to git you out with. Think about how I could maybe tell ye I've got to go find some wire cutters but not ever come back. How would you shoot me then? Think about that."

She was silent, thinking about it, he decided. He was a little amazed that she hadn't thought of it to begin with, that she would be dumb enough to try something like that. But maybe she wasn't dumb so much as desperate. Yes, she must be awful desperate to get out, he thought. He felt that made her look guiltier than ever. It rankled him some, the thought that what he'd taken for a nice lady might just be some fancy city woman coming up here to the hills to bilk some poor country people out of the money she'd stolen from their brothers after poisoning them and her tricking him into helping her rob his own kind of folks.

She was softly weeping. She sniffled and said, "Why don't you leave, then?"

"Naw," he said. "It's a while yet to dawn. Why don't you talk some?"

"About what?" she said.

"*Them*," he said.

CHAPTER 11

I remember very well (she said to him, by and by) the first day I saw them. It was late summer, nearly three years ago. My boarding house was a large white Victorian, three floors with cupolas and crockets and balustrades—it had been built by Mr. Cooper's, my husband's, family on Scott Street after the Reconstruction era of the last century. I like to think it was—I keep saying "was" instead of "is" because I won't ever run it anymore—that it was one of the better boarding houses in Little Rock, which is perhaps why I was somewhat chilly or even huffy when I opened the door that day in the late summer three years ago and saw these two men in their bib overalls and sweat-stained old felt hats, holding their cheap cardboard suitcases and with other odds and ends of their possessions wrapped in blankets. One of them—it was Denton—said that a fellow in a shoe store had told them they might find a room in my house.

When he mentioned the shoe store, I looked down at their feet and saw that both of them were wearing new shoes, black oxfords that were too good for overalls, but whichever shoe store, or whichever shoe salesman, he had been playing a joke on them by recommending my establishment. I thought at first that they might be transients connected with the North Little Rock Livestock Show, but then I realized that was not scheduled to open until the following month. As it happened, I did have a few vacant rooms—the economy was down that year, which I think was one reason they came to Little Rock to find work. You would have been already seventeen then, Hawk, so maybe you can remember if people were going hungry in this part of the country that year. Anyway, I *did* have room for more boarders, although I didn't know if I had room for *those* boarders. So I asked them for references.

Denton and Monroe looked at each other, and then they looked back at me, and Denton said, "References, ma'am?"

I told them that it was customary to present letters from the owners of previous establishments where they had boarded testifying to their character and sobriety and so forth.

Denton said that they had never boarded anywhere before, that up until then, they had always lived "up to home."

Monroe added that as far as sobriety was concerned, neither he nor his brother had ever touched a drop.

His mention of "brother" made me realize for the first time that the two men were brothers. Until then, I was assuming that the reason they looked so much alike is that all country people look alike. I guess it was from that moment that I began to realize that country people are not all alike.

These two men, for all their rustic appearance, seemed to me serious, able-bodied, and hard-working men; they seemed . . . well, *straight* is the word. I realized I could probably count on them to help mend a broken shutter or rake leaves in the fall. My only three men boarders at that time were an old jeweler, a one-armed bank clerk, and a rheumatic druggist. I could never depend on any of them to lend a hand around the house. So here were these two tall, strong middle-aged countrymen asking me if I had not rooms but *a* room—they were ready to share the same bed, if that's all I had.

Still I couldn't say yes just like that. So I showed them the available rooms and told them what I charged for room and two meals a day, and then I told them about a less expensive boarding house over on Cumberland Street and suggested that they go and have a look at that place and see if it wouldn't be better for them. They did but returned within a few minutes, and Denton said, "The lady there don't seem to want us," and I realized then that Mrs. Koger, who ran the other boarding house, must have been even more disdainful than I, and I felt sorry for having embarrassed the brothers at the same time that I had further doubts about accepting them. What would my other boarders think? In addition to the three men, five other boarders were women, three shop-girls and two teachers, none of them especially refined but still a class of people that might not welcome the brothers. The men's rooms were on the third floor, the women's on the second, while my rooms and the dining room were on the first, along with a common parlor. How would these Ingledew brothers look sitting in my parlor in their overalls, even if they had new black oxfords on their feet?

But, to be truthful, I needed the extra income. When my husband was killed in the war, I had to take over the management of the household finances, and when I converted our home into a boarding house, I figured carefully the exact number of boarders—ten—that I would need to "break even," that is, to pay for the food and upkeep, and to supplement the small widow's pension that the government paid me, and, of course, to pay the cook. No, I didn't do the cooking in my boarding house. I had a girl, Clarissa, a Negro, who had been our family cook before my husband went to the war, and afterwards, when I decided to convert our home into a boarding house, I asked her if she were willing to remain and to take on the extra burden of cooking for ten more people—at extra wages, of course—and she was glad to and was in fact a wonderful cook. I think, looking back, that it was her cooking which gave my house its reputation.

"What do you gentlemen like to eat?" I asked the Ingledew brothers, and they said they weren't "partial," that whatever was on the table was more than good enough for them.

"Where are you employed?" I asked. They said they weren't, yet, but hoped to find work as soon as they found a place to stay.

"How long do you plan to stay?" I asked. I did not like to have transient guests, and all my boarders at that time had been with me for a year or more.

Denton said, "As long as we have to," and I asked how long that would be, and he said, "As long as it takes a man to save up enough so he don't have to worry anymore." That to me sounded like a pretty long time, and it sounded also as if the brothers were thrifty in addition to their other virtues.

"Do you have anything now?" I asked, and as a final question: "Could you pay a week's room and board in advance?"

The brothers simultaneously reached for their wallets, and Denton said, "We can pay a month in advance, if you want."

"A week will do," I said. I later learned that the men had just finished their harvest here in Stay More; that's why they were leaving Stay More at that particular time of late summer, when most of their farm work had been finished and they had sold enough livestock to give them a nest egg for going to Little Rock.

So I told them to take their pick of whichever of the two rooms I had showed them and told them to move on in. The larger of the two rooms had two beds in it and had previously been occupied by one of the few couples I'd ever had at the boarding house, a traveling salesman and his wife who were frequently on the road and one day did not return from the road. The smaller room had only one large bed but was brighter and airier than the larger, and for this reason, I think, the brothers chose it. I offered to put another bed into the room, although that would have cramped it, but the brothers told me they had slept in the same bed since they were infants and were too old to change their ways now. It was nearly two years later before I learned that they wouldn't have minded having another bed in the room but were under the mistaken impression that I would have charged them extra for it. By that time, when I assured them I wouldn't charge for an extra bed, they said they had gotten used to sleeping in that one big bed.

At first, I wondered if the brothers might be . . . well, you know, *that* kind of man, and I wondered how it was that two such men, handsome in their rugged way, had never married. But it didn't take me long to discover how painfully shy they were, especially with women. They rarely spoke unless someone asked them a question. Apparently, from what I've gathered, shyness is practically a hereditary condition for Ingledew men. You know Willis, he's just like them. And John Ingledew's five sons—every one of them, unnaturally bashful or modest or retiring. There was one of my lady boarders, a schoolteacher, Miss Griffith, who was positively smitten with the Ingledew brothers from the beginning and was always flirting with them or trying to get their attention, never with any success, so she began teasing them, or perhaps she wasn't teasing, asking them, "Which of you shall marry me?" and things like that, until finally I had to speak to her about it—I'd rarely chastised a boarder except for flagrant dereliction in conduct or appearance, but I spoke to her privately and said, "Miss Griffith, can't you see how uncomfortable you're making those poor men?" And she replied, "Can't you see how uncomfortable they're making me? I can't get either one of them to notice me!" "Perhaps," I said, "they simply don't *want* to notice you." She said, "But that's insulting." "No," I said, "it isn't, and I must ask you to refrain from making such a glaring play for them." She left the room in a huff, calling back at me, "Saving them for yourself, eh?"

But from the very beginning, I was relieved that the other boarders as well as Miss Griffith didn't look down upon these men. None of them ever said anything to me to indicate displeasure that the men were sleeping in that house and eating with them at the table. Only one, the one-armed bank clerk, McKinna, sometimes would refer to them as "hillbillies" or "clodhoppers"—never in their presence, of course, and Mr. McKinna was a very irascible man who liked to pretend that he disliked every element of humanity; he referred to Clarissa as "that nigger hash burner" although he loved her food, and he always had such a ready insult for everyone that the other boarders called him "Muck Anna" behind his back. He was easy to dislike—last week, the police were rough in their handling of him when they were subjecting all of us to their "third degree."

I remember the first evening the Ingledews came, right after supper, when they were stuffed and delighted—obviously, they'd never had that much food, or that much good food, at one sitting before—I overheard them talking to each other on the porch about how all they needed now was a big cigar, and then one of them, Denton, came to me and asked where he could buy a cigar, and I was about to send him down the street to the lobby of one of the hotels when I realized the frowns or stares he might get going into a hotel in his overalls, so I told him that in celebration of their coming to our boarding house, I would give them a couple of cigars, and I went back into my quarters and then sneaked out the rear door and down the street to the hotel, where I bought two of the largest cigars they had and came back. And the brothers just sat out on the porch, smoking their cigars and obviously feeling like kings. From the way they held their cigars, it seemed to me they had never held one before. Neither of them actually smoked very much on a regular basis—a pipe now and then—and both of them seemed to get a little queasy from the cigars. But I'll always remember the picture of them that first evening, sitting there in the wicker chairs on my front porch, smoking their cigars and waving at the passersby . . . until Denton pointed out to Monroe that none of the other boarders were waving at passersby, so maybe you don't do that sort of thing in the city.

The next morning, at the breakfast table, they declared that they were going out to look for work. Mr. Frommler, the old German jeweler, asked them what sort of work they were looking for. They said they could do anything that could be done with two hands. "Can you cut a diamond? Replace a mainspring?" Mr. Frommler asked them, and they said no, they allowed as how there might be a lot of things done with two hands which they couldn't do. Mr. McKinna, the one-armed bank clerk, was becoming sensitive about this talk of two hands, and he asked them, "Can you operate an adding machine?" They both looked at him and noticed the stub of his missing arm, and then they blushed and coughed and said there were probably a lot of things they couldn't do with either hand.

No, the brothers had large hands, powerful hands, good for manual labor in the city but little else, and if they hoped to save any money, they could never do it on the wages paid manual labor. Then too, their ages—both men were approaching fifty—were against them in their search for employment. They had hoped, at first, to find jobs together in the same place, but that didn't happen. After two days of walking the streets, out to the East End factory district and back, Denton found a job with a meat packer, unloading heavy carcasses of beef and pork, but they had no room for Monroe. It took almost a week for Monroe to find his job, with a plate-glass company, carrying and installing heavy sheets of glass. Although they both worked hard, I think it took them a while to get adjusted—or maybe they never got adjusted—to the idea of working for somebody else. All their lives, they, like most of your people in this part of the country, even if poor, considered themselves landed gentry working for them-selves. Then, in Little Rock, they became "hired hands," even if they were producing more income in a month than they could have in a year back home. They talked about that, to each other, sitting on the porch, and I would overhear them.

But both men worked hard, and their employers liked them and gave them periodic raises, and within a year, both men moved up: Denton became foreman of the receiving department at the meat packer's, while Monroe became head glazier at the plate-glass company. When a vacancy developed in Denton's department, he tried to persuade Monroe to come to work for him, and likewise, when there was an opening at Monroe's company, he tried to hire Denton, but the brothers had discovered a cer-tain advantage in working for different companies: it gave them more to talk about when they were together.

They did a lot of talking with each other. That was about all they did. To my knowledge, they never read anything, not even the newspaper. Of course, they never went to the theater. Nor to church. I don't think Denton and Monroe were atheists. I talked with them once, briefly, about religion. Religion to them was simply a habit, like whiskey drinking, which they had not happened to acquire. On Sundays, when the weather was good, they would walk over to City Park and loaf around on the benches until some of the other men would organize a "pickup" baseball game. Denton and Monroe were both, despite their ages, very good at baseball. Recently, I went with them a number of times and watched. Denton was a hitter, and many times, I've seen him knock the ball out of the park and across the street onto somebody's porch . . . or through their window, in which case Monroe would offer to replace the glass free of charge before sun-down. Monroe was a pitcher, and practically the only person who could hit a ball thrown by him was Denton. The other men would try to get them on opposing teams, but they always played on the same team, and that team always won. Always. They never lost a single game. I asked Monroe once if that wasn't kind of monotonous, winning every time, but he just said, "It aint no fun to lose."

For their other amusements, they went to all the livestock shows and, occasionally, a rodeo in North Little Rock, and one time, Mr. McKinna invited them to go with him to Hot Springs to watch the horse races, and although they went, they didn't place any bets, because gambling was another habit they had never acquired and didn't want to. Sometimes, about once a month, they would go for a long walk southeast of the city to the farm country, where they would just stroll down the country lanes, looking at people's barns and livestock and waving if they saw anybody and being waved at in return. I went with them once not too long ago. We must have hiked eight or nine miles, and I was completely worn out when we got back, but they could have walked another eight or nine. But it was an educational experience for me, one or both of them pointing out things of interest and explaining them. I've always been a city girl; I grew up in Memphis and have spent most of my life in Little Rock. In fact, I think that was the first time I'd ever been for a long walk in the country.

They were homesick a lot, of course. From the beginning, that was the main thing they talked about. They would sit on the porch of my house every evening after supper and reminisce about Stay More. They were talking only to each other, but anybody who happened to be sitting on the porch could listen in. They told old tales, reworked old legends, rehashed their entire boyhoods, and analyzed the character of every citizen of Stay More in complete detail. After three years of overhearing their talk, I felt almost as if I had been born here and knew the whole town. Recently, they had been talking about bringing me up here for a visit . . . I was . . . I was looking forward to it very much. I . . . I brought them here instead.

But they never came back until then. I don't think it was because they couldn't afford it, and of course, their employers offered them the standard week's vacation with pay each year, which they declined. I can only think of what Denton said that first day I met them, that they intended to stay in Little Rock "as long as it takes a man to save up enough so he don't have to worry anymore." Maybe that day was not too far off. I think . . . I wonder if, when they invited me to visit Stay More with them, they were getting ready to ask me if . . .

Oh, I'm being foolish and speculative! But anyway, they saved their money carefully. They paid for their room and board promptly upon returning from work every Saturday evening, but that was about all they spent. In three years, they each bought two changes of clothes and two pairs of shoes. Nothing else, except a very small quantity of pipe tobacco or twenty-five-cent tickets to the rodeo. With no wives or children to support, they could save, out of their foremen's wages, almost $6,000. Mr. McKinna tried to persuade them to deposit their savings in an account at his bank, but they wouldn't. Nobody knew where they were keeping it . . . until recently, when they told me they had been mailing it regularly in postal money orders to their brother Willis in Stay More, who deposited it in their brother John's bank. But I guess that sounds incriminating, doesn't it? That sounds as if I poisoned them as soon as I found out where the money was. But if that were my motive, why would I have told John they had been poisoned? Why would I have given away the cause of their deaths?

When they died, my first thought was that John might have embezzled their money and, when he learned that they were coming back to Stay More to visit, come to Little Rock and killed them. Or possibly, Willis had never deposited their money but cashed the postal money orders in his own post office and kept the money. I thought that one or the other of them must be guilty. That's why I came here. I never suspected Drussie until today.

You aren't saying anything, Hawk. You're sure I'm guilty, aren't you? Do I have to talk to you about personal matters? Do I have to tell you how the brothers came to feel for me and I for them? So you will believe that I couldn't have killed them? It began last winter, when I was seriously ill and had to be hospitalized for a time. When I was convalescing at the hospital, some of my boarders sent me flowers. Mr. Shepherd sent a box of candy from his drugstore. Mr. Frommler sent me a silver brooch from his shop. I almost expected Mr. McKinna to send a banknote from his bank, but he didn't send anything. Except for him, they all sent me something, yet none of them came to visit me—maybe they thought my disease was contagious, which it was not—none of them came to visit except Denton and Monroe.

Well, as I say, they were extremely shy men. In the two and a half years they had lived with me at that time, they had rarely spoken to me unless it was something like "Could you pass the salt, please?" or "Here's my board money." But as soon as the hospital permitted visitors to my room, there they were. They came in and said, "How you feel?" and then took chairs and sat down and just sat there, not talking. I was still very weak at the time, too tired to talk really, so I was glad in a way that they were not talking. They were just *there*, and I was glad of that—that two people thought enough of me to keep me company when I was bedridden. They didn't bring me anything except themselves. I later learned from Monroe that this is a custom of your people, that country folks always "sit up with the sick"—not in the fashion of visiting with them, but merely of being with them. Under other circumstances, I would have been very uncomfortable to have a man sitting in silence beside my bed, but I was not uncomfortable then—I was happy.

They came every day. Together or one by one in shifts. I was never alone during visiting hours, and these were, as I recall, from two to four in the afternoon and from seven to nine in the evening. As I began to recover, I said they shouldn't leave their jobs in the afternoon to come and visit, but they just replied that they'd never taken a vacation and had some free time coming to them. They came, one or the other or both, twice a day, every day for the thirteen days that I remained in the hospital, and when I was well enough to leave, they hired a taxicab, and I sat between them to ride home.

Oh, of course, they were not silent *all* that time that they were in my hospital room. They brought me bits of news about the "outside world" and kept me assured that everything was all right at the boarding house in my absence, and they even collected the weekly rent from the other boarders and brought it to me along with their own, and they would tell me little anecdotes they had picked up at work, and during the evening visiting hours, when they usually came together, they would sit and reminisce with each other about Stay More in their usual fashion, and I would listen with interest and sometimes ask a question.

I'm afraid I wasn't much to look at. My illness had left me thin and pale and looking much older than my years. But the first thing one or the other of them usually said whenever he came at visiting time was something like "You're shore lookin purty today, Miz Cooper." And then they stopped calling me "Miz Cooper" and began to call me "Emily" or "Em." And then, the last week I was in the hospital, each of them, whenever he was leaving, would lean down and lightly kiss my forehead. Once, one of them kissed my cheek.

I wasn't well when I left the hospital, but I had stayed as long as I could afford to. I had to remain in bed at home for another two weeks before I could really get up and move around again, and during those two weeks, they continued to "visit" me, although a few of the other boarders would also come into my room and sit for a while, but in a very self-conscious way that was not at all like the brothers'.

Denton and Monroe were always doing little things for me and asking if there was anything I needed and making sure that I was always comfortable. Clarissa, the cook, teased me about it. She would say, "Dem boys sho got it sweet fo you, Missy."

But I don't really know how much of it was from affection. Once I asked them, "Why are you being so nice to me?" but they just answered, "You been nice to us." Whatever it was, I felt closer to those two men than I ever had toward anyone. For you to understand, I'd have to tell you about my father and my brother and George Cooper, the man I married, and I don't have time to tell you about them.

Once, when Monroe was visiting my room and got up to leave and came and leaned down to kiss my cheek, I turned my head toward him so that his lips touched mine. He blushed very deeply and left the room quickly, but the next time he visited by himself, he left his kiss between my cheek and my mouth. And so did Denton, when he came. After that, they always came separately.

But when I was well enough to walk, they came together and told me I needed sunshine and fresh air, and they marched me between them to the City Park, where I sat between them on a bench for a long time and then remained to watch them play their baseball game. One of the wives of the other players came and sat beside me and said, "They are sure showing off for you today, honey," and I realized then that they were, that Monroe struck out every batter he faced in a—what do you call it?—a "no-hitter," and Denton, every time he went to bat, knocked the ball over the trees and across the street. I felt as if I were a schoolgirl, not as if they were men of fifty-one and fifty-two and I a widow of thirty-seven—there, I've slipped and given away my age—but as if all of us were teenagers. It was a strange but a wonderful feeling—and the really strange thing is that we were, in a way, for the short while it lasted, transformed again into youths. They were not middle-aged bachelors acting silly around a widow but shy young boys too timid to tell their girl how they felt about her but not too timid nearly to break their necks showing her what great baseball players they were.

Once—thank God it was *only* once—they even fought over me. We were at the park on a weekday, which they had taken off as more of their "vacation" to see to it that I got plenty of sunshine and fresh air, and on weekdays, there are no other men in the park to play baseball, so Denton and Monroe played a game against each other, Monroe pitching and Denton hitting. It went on and on in almost a kind of deadlock. Denton would either strike out or hit the ball over the trees. This went on for so long, without either of them proving superiority, that they began to lose patience, and finally, Denton accused Monroe of trying to "bean" him, and they squared off and picked a fight and began knocking each other around. I tried to intercede, but they wouldn't stop to listen. Neither of them won the fight either. They simply got exhausted and quit and shook hands, Denton saying, "No sense us gittin kilt," and Monroe saying, "Let's not fight again." Then they walked me home between them, I holding an arm of each.

I never favored one over the other. It would have been impossible. There were scarcely any differences between them: maybe Monroe was a little more gallant, maybe Denton a little more intelligent, maybe Monroe slightly better looking, maybe Denton slightly stronger. If one of them had ever asked me to marry him—and I seriously doubt that either of them would ever have gotten up enough nerve to—I would have had to marry both, or neither.

Now, that is all I'm going to tell you, Hawk. One or the other, or both of them, was with me almost constantly from then until the morning last week when they did not appear at the breakfast table, and I went to their room and found them, thinking at first that they were still sleeping and going to give their shoulders a shake, finding that they were asleep forever.

CHAPTER 12

Hock looked out the eastern window of the bank and saw that the sun had risen. Looking out the window, he noticed that one of its four panes was missing and remembered that he had broken it. He took a wastebasket and knelt and picked the pieces of glass off the floor and put them in the wastebasket, then went behind the teller's counter and put the wastebasket behind it, under it. Then he took his pocketknife and began to gouge out the putty from around one of the windowpanes on a less conspicuous window behind the counter. He removed the pane intact, covering the hole by hanging a calendar over it. He found the glazing points from the broke pane and used them to hold the pane in place. It was a crude job, but anybody coming to the bank would not see that a window light had been busted. Emily Cooper, he noticed, was not watching him replace the window. She sat with her head in her hands, staring at the floor.

As he was finishing the window, he looked through it and saw two people coming up the road, a man and a woman. He waited until they were close enough for him to identify them—it was Willis Ingledew and his sister, Drussie, who was carrying a basket—and then he went behind the teller's counter and crouched beneath it. "Comp'ny's comin," he said to Emily. He scrooched back into the darkest corner of the counter.

The side door opened. "Mornin," he heard Willis Ingledew say, then Drussie said, "We brung ye some breakfust." He heard a key turn in the lock of the wire cage, and Willis said, "Don't try to git out. We'll pass it in to you." Then Hock heard the gate close and the lock snap.

Drussie said, "Reckon yo're narvous it's got pizen in it, huh? Wal, if you really kilt our brothers, pizenin's too good fer ye."

Hock could not hear if Emily said anything.

Willis said, "John's goin up to Jasper directly, to fetch the sheriff. Reckon they'll be here afore noon. If they aint, we'll bring ye some dinner. I'll leave that there side door unlocked so they kin git in when they come." Hock heard them move to the door and open it.

Drussie said, "Law, what's ole Horace settin yonder fer?"

"Reckon he thinks he's guardin the bank," Willis said.

They went away, and Hock came out from under the counter and tested the door and saw that Willis had actually left it unlocked. Well, at least Hock wouldn't have any trouble getting *out* of the bank.

"Come and eat, Hawk," she invited. "I'll bet you're starved."

"I could eat a horse, hide and all," he said and laughed. "But how am I going to get into there where the food's at?"

"Why don't you get some wire cutters?" she suggested.

"In broad daylight?" he said. "And didn't you notice how I bothered to put another winder light up where I broke that'un?"

"Well, come here," she said. "I can feed you through the wire."

He was sure hungry, all right. The last meal he'd had was supper day before yesterday. He went up close to the wire cage, and Emily Cooper cut off a piece of her fried egg and speared it on her fork and passed the fork tines through the mesh of the wire, and Hock bit the egg off of it. She did the same for the sausage and biscuits.

"Aint you eatin any of it, yoreself?" he asked.

"I'm not hungry," she said. "You can have it all. But I don't know how I could get this coffee out to you."

"I'll rig up a straw," he said and took a deposit slip from the teller's counter and rolled it into a tube. Emily held the Mason jar of coffee against the wire, and he poked one end of the tube into it and sucked on the other. The coffee was very hot and burned his tongue. "Let it cool a spell," he said.

Bite by bite, she fed him the rest of the eggs, sausage, and biscuit, and by then, the coffee had cooled down enough for him to drink it through his straw.

Breakfast finished, he said with satisfaction, "It shore makes a difference, not havin a empty belly. I'm much obliged to ye."

A thought occurred to him. What if Drussie had poisoned that breakfast? If she were really the guilty one and had poisoned the brothers, maybe she had tried to poison Emily Cooper. But Emily hadn't eaten any of it. Did Emily too think it might be poisoned? Is that why she didn't eat any of it? Hock's stomach was churning, and he wondered if he ought to try to throw up. But no, he couldn't believe that Emily would let him eat poisoned food. And more than that, he couldn't believe that Drussie Ingledew would have poisoned her brothers.

"You won't get me out, before the sheriff comes?" Emily asked him.

"I'm still a-studyin on it," Hock said. "I aint made up my mind one way or th'other. If yo're innocent, like ye say, why don't you jist talk with the sheriff about it?"

She chuckled an ironic laugh. "Hawk," she said, "if a nice boy like you won't believe me, what do you think the sheriff will feel?"

"Wal," he said. "Tell me a few things. Tell me how them police down to Little Rock was persuaded ye didn't do it."

"They ransacked my house. They made tests. They asked me a thousand questions. They asked the other boarders hundreds of questions."

"Was anybody with the Ingledew brothers on the night before—I mean the night before the morning you found them?"

"Only me . . . until my bedtime. Usually I retire quite early, an hour or so before Denton and Monroe. I don't know who might have been with them after I went to bed."

"Was any of the other boarders still up when you went to bed?"

"Most of them were. Mr. Frommler was in his room, reading. Miss Griffith was washing her hair. Mr. McKinna was in the parlor, working on his account books."

"And the brothers was out on the porch, by theirselfs?"

"Yes."

"Did any of them boarders, Frommler or McKinna or Miz Griffith, gener'ly talk much lately to the Ingledews?"

"You're sounding exactly like the Little Rock police questioning me."

"Well, did they?"

"Not Miss Griffith, certainly. She had long since given up her flirtation with them. Mr. Frommler sometimes sat on the porch with them at night, but he wasn't sitting with them *that* night, and I wish I had never mentioned it to the police, because they nearly gave him a nervous breakdown with their questions."

"What about McKinna?"

"Mr. McKinna talked to them occasionally. He was a rather patronizing man, always full of suggestions to them about how they should invest their savings and manage their affairs. I mentioned to the police that Mr. McKinna had invited Denton and Monroe to the Hot Springs horse races one day back in March. Denton and Monroe went with him but only to watch the horses race. They said they didn't place any bets. Mr. McKinna didn't invite them again. The police questioned him thoroughly but could find no evidence that he got any money from them or would have had any motive for murdering them."

Hock thought that over. If he had been a policeman, he would have been just a *little* bit rougher on this McKinna feller. "What happened to all them people?" Hock asked. "I mean, are they still stayin at yore house?"

"No. Some of them, particularly the women, moved out at once, horrified to remain in a house where two murders had occurred. I was grief stricken and could not very well go on with the maintenance of a boarding house. Within a few days, all the boarders had left, and Mrs. Koger offered Clarissa a job as cook in her boarding house, so I closed my house and put it on the market. It was a desirable property and was purchased immediately."

Hock thought that over. There was just one or two more questions that he could think of to ask. "What about Miss Griffith? You don't think she might've poisoned 'em, jist out of pure spite?"

"I thought of that, and so did the police, but we dismissed it. The circumstances weren't sufficient to warrant it. You need a stronger motive or else have to be deranged. She wasn't."

"Did the Ingledews ever fool around with anybody else in Little Rock? I mean, did they 'sociate with any gamblers, say, or shady characters or what all?"

"No. The police checked that carefully and investigated the meat packer where Denton worked and the glass company where Monroe worked. As I said, they weren't gamblers. There's no evidence that Denton and Monroe had any dealings with anyone."

"So them police jist gave up?"

"No, the case is still open, but they don't seem to have much hope of finding any clues."

"What do you think them police would do if they knew that the brothers left all their money to you?"

"They would, I'm sure, lock me up and ask me another thousand questions."

Hock thought that over. How could he possibly turn her loose if the Little Rock police would lock her up? Hock began to pace the floor of the bank, doing his thinking. But he couldn't decide what to do.

When he asked her no further questions, nor said anything, she said to him, "Well, Mr. Sheriff, what is your verdict?"

"I don't believe you done it, Emily," he said.

"Then get me out of here!" she said.

Where could he get wire cutters in broad daylight? Try to sneak around through the back of Willis's store? That was too risky. He began examining the cage, checking the way it was fastened to the walls and floor and ceiling. At the walls, the ends of the wires were embedded into cement mortar. But on the floor, the wire was attached to brackets that were held with screws into the wood floor. He took out his pocketknife and knelt on the floor.

As he was kneeling there with the pocketknife, there came a knock at the front door. Hock sprang up, but it was too late; he had already been spotted by the man peering through the front window. *Second damn time,* he thought, *second damn time that I've been caught trying to get into this cage.* Well, he told himself, he hadn't opened it either time, and maybe the man couldn't tell that he'd been trying to open it. Who was the man? The sheriff?

He went to the door and looked through the glass at the man. If he was the sheriff, why wasn't John Ingledew with him? The man wore a black suit. He didn't much look like a sheriff. One sleeve of the suit was doubled back and fastened with a safety pin at the shoulder. A one-armed sheriff?

Hock couldn't open this door. He spoke through it: "Yeah? Could I help you?"

"Is this the bank?"

"Yeah, are you a customer?"

"Yes. Are you open?"

"Will be soon," Hock replied. "I'm jist the janitor. But you'll have to come around to the side door to git in."

"All right," the man said and began walking across the porch to the side of the building.

Hock returned quickly to the cage and saw that Emily had turned around with her back to the door. She was sitting at the desk as if she were working on papers there.

"Did you see him?" Hock asked.

"I caught a glimpse of him before I turned away. I don't think he saw me."

"Is it McKinna?"

"I'm sure of it."

"What's he here for?"

"I don't know, but we're going to find out. Would you recognize me from the back, like this?"

Hock studied her back and decided that she could pass for just about anybody from the back.

"I reckon not," he said.

"Would ye recognize mah voice if ah tawked lak this?" she said. It didn't sound to Hock like anything he'd heard, but it didn't sound like her either.

"Ah reckon not," he said.

"All right," she said. "Let him in."

CHAPTER 13

Hock opened the side door and let the man come into the bank.

"This *is* the Swains Creek Bank and Trust Company, isn't it?" the man asked. "There's no sign out front."

"No need of a sign," Hock said. "Everbody hereabouts knows it's the bank anyhow." He jerked his thumb at the wire cage. "That there is Miz Wilson, our teller. She's purty busy right now. Could I help ye?"

"Not if you're just the janitor," the man said, with a disdainful expression. He was sure a mean-looking sonofabitch, Hock decided. If I wanted to hire me a poisoner, I'd offer him first crack at the job. The man declared, "I have two certified checks that I want to cash." The man used his one hand to take a handkerchief from his pocket and mop his brow with it. "I've had to walk all the way from Jasper, and I'm in a hurry. You people don't have much of a transportation system in these wild and wooly backwoods." The man looked disdainfully around the room. "Are you sure this is the bank? It doesn't look like one. I'm a banker myself; I should know. What's the cage for? And what's your teller doing inside it?"

"She'll tend to ye directly," Hock said and went behind the teller's counter and found a dustrag and began dusting the countertop with it.

Emily Cooper spoke without turning. "Yeeah? Whut is it?"

The man moved closer to her cage. "I'd like to cash two checks."

"How much?" she said, still imitating—or trying to—a hill woman's voice.

"They total roughly six thousand dollars," he said.

"Heaven sakes!" she exclaimed, still not turning. "That's a heap o money!"

"They are certified checks," he declared.

"Who they drawn on?"

"Denton Ingledew and Monroe Ingledew."

"Let's see them," she said in her own voice and turned, and when she turned around to face him, she was holding her revolver in one hand.

Hock was watching the man closely. At first, his face just seemed blank, and then, for a very long instant, he just looked puzzled, but then suddenly, his eyes nearly popped out of his head, his jaw hung open, his legs crumbled, and he staggered to the counter and managed to prop himself up with one arm. In a weak voice, he croaked, "Emily Cooper!"

"Let's see them," she said again. "Hawk, take his checks."

Hock held out his hand for the checks, and when the man was slow in reaching for his wallet, Hawk snarled, "You heard her, buster! Get 'em out!"

Almost absently, as if not able to give full thought to the futility of the gesture, the man took out his wallet and withdrew the checks from it and handed them to Hock. Hock took them to the cage, where Emily, keeping her gun on the man, read the checks.

"You monster," she said. "Did you forge their signatures?"

"I did not," he said. "Their signatures are authentic."

"Why didn't you cash them in the bank you work for?"

"Because the money is in *this* bank. What are *you* doing here? And why are you in that cage? And above all, why are you pointing that weapon at me?"

"I think you know the answer to that question yourself."

The man was sweating profusely. "Perhaps you weren't aware of it, Mrs. Cooper, but the brothers were deeply in debt to me as a result of their gambling losses at the Hot Springs track."

"That wasn't what you told the police," she said.

"I saw no reason to. They would naturally have sought to connect it with the brothers' death, when you and I know—don't we?—that the brothers killed themselves in despair over losing all their savings. I'm sorry, of course, they did that, but a debt is a debt, and—"

"Shut up, you mealymouthed bastard!" she said. It was the first time Hock had heard her swear. It didn't sound ladylike, but Hock admired the way she could do it. There was a long moment of silence, which she ended by saying, "Do you have anything decent to say before you die?"

The man stole a glance at the door. Hock moved to stand between the man and the door. The man glared at him. "Who are you?" the man demanded of him. "What's your involvement in this matter?"

"I'm Hawk Tuttle," he said. "Newton County deputy sheriff."

The man was startled but said, "Where's your badge?"

"We'uns don't flash badges hereabouts," Hock said and showed the man his fists. "These here are our badge."

"If you are an officer, then you must believe me when I say that I am no more guilty of the Ingledews' deaths than this woman is. What is she doing, anyway? How did she get into that cage?"

"I locked her up there," Hock said. "Until you showed up, she was the prime suspect."

"Oh? Was she making a claim for the money too?"

"She wasn't makin no claim fer it, buster. It was *willed* to her. The Ingledews left it to her in their wills."

The man stared at Emily. His one hand was trembling considerably. "Very clever of you, Mrs. Cooper. So they were not suicides, after all. You poisoned them. But the joke is on you, then. For that money which they willed to you was not theirs to will. It was mine."

Emily Cooper replied, "You aren't sounding like a man who is about to die. Why don't you express regrets? You may even pray if you like."

The man turned to Hock. "You aren't going to let her shoot me, are you? Goddammit, why is she armed in the first place? How did you let her get that gun?"

"I didn't know she had it," Hock said. "Reckon she must've sneaked it in her purse."

"You stupid hayseed law officers don't even have the sense to search a person before locking them up? And what is worse, aren't you armed yourself? Can't you stop her from shooting me? Am I not entitled to a fair trial?"

Hock turned to her. "Emily," he said, "are you honestly fixin to shoot him?"

"Of course."

"Hadn't ye orter wait and let the sheriff talk to 'im?"

"Justice in a court of law is very slow, and as you can see, he's a very slick talker. It would be my word against his. Hawk, I *know* he did it now. I haven't the slightest doubt. This 'check' business proves it. I'm sure Denton and Monroe weren't lying to me when they said they didn't gamble at the Hot Springs track."

"But they did!" Mr. McKinna protested. He extended his one arm in a beseeching gesture to Hock. "You have to believe me. As she says, it's my word against hers. Indeed it is, and I know what I'm talking about. You aren't going to let her execute me without a trial, are you? What kind of backcountry justice is that?"

"You might as well know," Emily Cooper said to Mr. McKinna, "since you are about to die anyway, that he isn't really a deputy sheriff. Tell him you're not, Hawk."

"That's the way it goes, mister," Hock said.

The man seemed on the verge of fainting. "Emily, for God's sake!"

he beseeched her. "Can't we work out a deal? Instead of one or both of us getting in trouble with these backcountry yokels, couldn't we agree to splitting the money? Our first job is to get the money, and if we work together, we can persuade these clods to let us have it."

Emily's voice was very cold. "Denton and Monroe were just 'clods' too, weren't they? That's why you thought you could get away with your little scheme so easily. They were just 'backcountry yokels' to you. But to me, Mr. McKinna, they were wonderful men. I loved them. Did you know that?" She paused, and when he made no reply, she said in a matter-of-fact voice, "And as for the money, I already have it. In a check more negotiable than those two pieces of worthless paper."

The man stared at her for a moment and then glanced at Hock. Suddenly, his one hand came up and shoved hard against Hock's chest, pushing him backward.

"Out of my way!" he said and made for the door.

Emily fired. Her first shot hit him in the back of the neck. He reached for the doorknob but fell. Her second shot went into his ribs. Her third shot was deflected by the wire of the cage, which it cut through. Her fourth shot went into the small of McKinna's back, and her fifth shot into his head.

"Hold it," Hock said. "He's dead enough, and I just thought of somethin. Use your last shot on the lock of that cage."

She held the revolver in both hands and pointed it toward the keyhole in the lock and squeezed the trigger. Hock ripped the gate open and said, "Wal, I don't reckon you keer to wait fer the sheriff."

"I don't," she said and pointed at McKinna's hand. The dead man was tightly clutching the two worthless checks. "Those ought to explain things to the sheriff. Let's go."

"Jist a second," Hock said. From his pocket, he took the fifteen dollars that Tull Ingledew had paid him and wrote on a deposit slip, "FER DIPOZZIT OV TULL INGLEDOO," and left it with the money on the teller's counter.

Then he opened the side door. People were running up the road from the village toward the bank. Probably, they'd heard the sound of the shots.

"Let's run," Hock said to her. He took her hand and led her around behind the bank and up the mountain into the woods. They kept in the woods until they were well out of sight of the village. Hock looked back and saw that Horace was following them. "Aw, go on home, Horace," he said. "It's all over now." But the dog just wagged his tail and resumed following them. "That's the dog what found your other shoe," he explained to Emily Cooper. "He's a right nice old dog, and he likes me."

"Whose is he?" she asked.

"Aw, I reckon he's supposed to be Drussie's, but she don't much seem to care." He spoke again to Horace. "Dog, do ye aim to keep on followin me? I'm a-goin all the way to Pettigrew. You want to follow me over there and be my dog?" Horace wagged his tail. "Wal, come on then, Horace, let's go."

The three of them came down off the mountain north of the village, looked both ways up the road, then darted across and through the field into a thicket of trees that bordered the creek. They moved up Swains Creek behind the screen of the trees until they could find a spot where stepping stones were set into the shallow water. He went first across the stones, turning and helping her step from one to the other. He noticed for the first time she was barefoot; he should have remembered to pick up her shoes back at the bank.

They crossed the creek and were swallowed up by the woods on the other side. Keeping near but not on the trail that Hock remembered taking from the farm several miles to the west where he had left his mules and wagon, they hiked on through the woods with Horace trotting sometimes ahead and sometimes behind. Emily's bare feet became scratched and sore. He took off his shoes and insisted that she wear them; although several sizes too large, they were better than nothing. When she protested, "But what about you?" he pointed out that he had spent most of his life going barefoot; in fact, until recently, he had owned no shoes, only a pair of boots that he wore in the winter.

So they went on to the farm in the hamlet of Sidehill. He had her wait with Horace out of sight down the road while he retrieved his wagon, thanking the farmer for letting him pasture his mules and apologizing for having left them there longer than he intended. Then he hitched the mules to the wagon and drove down the road and picked up Emily Cooper. "Hop up, Horace." He gestured for the dog to get into the back of the wagon. "If you're goin the rest of the way with us, jump aboard." The dog hesitated for just a moment, then clambered across the tailgate into the wagon. Hock clucked to the mules, and they went on.

"Could be the sheriff will be out lookin fer us on the road to Pettigrew," Hock declared. "I reckon maybe we orter take the long way around." So he drove toward Boxley instead of Fallsville, and Hock hoped there would be a road going west or southwest from Boxley that would get them back into Madison County.

They talked to each other during the ride, but it was mostly chitchat. At one point, Hock remarked, "Y'know, I'm shore glad it wasn't one of the Ingledews, or any other of them people, as far as that goes. I'm glad it was a furriner and not one of us."

Emily Cooper just looked at him and couldn't seem to find anything to say about that.

They got as far as Kingston, back in Madison County, before nightfall, and Hock had a third or fourth cousin who lived in Kingston and gave them a place to stay for the night and supper. Hock didn't tell the family anything about Stay More; he just said that Mrs. Cooper had hired him to drive her around the countryside.

They drove on early the next day and reached Pettigrew shortly after noon. He took a back road to his house and introduced Emily Cooper to his mother. "Ma, this here's the lady I drove to Stay More. Funeral and all took us a while is why we didn't git back till today."

"Git in the house, quick!" his mother said, and when they were inside the house, she told him, "They's depity sher'fs from Newton County and Madison County both waitin down at the train station. What on earth have you'uns been up to?"

"Aw," Hock said, "we jist had a little trouble over to Stay More."

"You didn't kill a feller by any chance, did ye?"

"*I* didn't," he said.

"Anyhow, they're waitin down at the station fer ye," she said. "You shore caint put the lady on the train."

"We'll have to go on to the next station at St. Paul," Hock declared.

Emily Cooper asked, "Isn't that a long way?"

"Jist ten mile or so," Hock said.

"You'uns et yet?" his mother asked. "Stay to dinner."

His mother served them a fine dinner and put some supper for Hock into a sack with another Mason jar of milk. Hock and Emily got into the wagon again, and Hock called to his mother, "Look fer me when you see me."

"Be keerful," his mother said.

Hock took a back road that avoided the village and the train station but rejoined the St. Paul Road west of Pettigrew. "I don't reckon they'll be waitin at the St. Paul station too," he said.

They drove on and reached St. Paul in the late afternoon.

As the road dropped down into the White River valley, where the village was nestled up against the hills, Hock asked her, "Are you goin back to Little Rock?"

"No," she said. "I could never live there again."

"Where you goin, then?" he asked.

"I don't know. I have a sister in California. I've been thinking about visiting her for a while. I've never been out there."

"I hear it's a right purty place," Hock said.

"Would you like to go?" she asked.

He studied it. Was she offering him an invitation to take him way out there? He smiled at the thought of that, but he said, "Pettigrew's my home."

"Well," she said.

They drove into St. Paul, a sizable village that was the second largest town in Madison County, after Huntsville, and Emily Cooper said, "I'd like to buy some shoes and other things."

"There's a mercantile store over yonder," Hock said, pointing down the street. He clucked at his mules and drove on to the store.

"Come in with me," she invited him. He did, and when they were inside the store, she said, "I'd like to buy you some clothes."

He looked down at himself. His shirt and trousers and shoes were old and had once belonged to his father. But he said, "You don't have to do that."

"But I want to," she said.

"I kin make do with what I've got," he said.

"You've done so much for me," she said. "It's the least I can do for you."

It was her third offer; to decline that would be final. "Well, maybe I could use another shirt," he allowed.

"Get whatever you want," she said, and he looked at all the shirts and tried to pick one out. He couldn't make up his mind between two nice-looking shirts, so she made him get both of them. Then she persuaded him to buy a keen pair of trousers. And some fine blucher shoes. For herself, she bought a suitcase and a dress and a hat and some underclothes and a pair of shoes. The shoes, he noticed, were black patent leather with a bit of paisley at vamp, strap, and quarter. He laughed. "Like them kind, do ye?" he observed.

"Sentimental reasons," she said with a smile.

She paid for all the clothes, and he drove her on to the St. Paul railway station. There he learned that only one train a week was running now and that the last one had departed two days before.

"Oh dear," she said when he told her.

"Well, heck," he said. "I've come this fur. I kin take ye on to Fayetteville. I've always wanted to see that town. Hear it's the biggest town in this part of the country."

"But that's a far way," she said.

"It aint as fur as Californy," he said, and got back into the wagon and clucked once more to his mules, and they turned into the road that follows the long curving sweep of the White River down toward Fayetteville.

STORIES

⚡⚡⚡

A Second Career

FRAMED IN THE DIAMOND-PANED WINDOW of his study, the church lay in its blackened granite cumbersomeness beneath a gray March sky; on its maze of cornices, pigeons congregated out of the raw wind and added their droppings to the maculate facade of the meetinghouse. Young Reverend Winstead turned his back on this bleak view, hunched over his desk, forced the church from his mind (it was Thursday morning, his Sunday sermon was written, none of his flock were sick this day), and, armed with nothing but a vision or ambition and a gold-tipped Parker pen (gift of National Burial & Life, whose name was printed in unobtrusive gold letters along the shank), began to write:

"Arthur Manning, a pillar of the church financially if not spiritually, came in person to the parsonage one afternoon and confronted Reverend Norris with an extraordinary problem. His only child, Karen, a quiet, lovely thing of fifteen, had suddenly been stricken with leukemia, and her doctors had told Arthur Manning that the young lady could hope for no more than a year of life. Now, Manning was a man of imagination and conscience as well as wealth, so he had broken the tragic news to Karen by softening it somewhat with the announcement that she could have anything she wanted—a trip to Europe, a stable of horses, an expensive sports car, anything . . .

"'Do you know what she wants?' Manning asked rhetorically of Reverend Norris, ignoring the coffee which the minister had poured for him. 'I offered that girl anything that money can buy. Anything, mind you, that money can buy. Do you know what she wants?'

"'What?' Reverend Norris gently inquired.

"'A baby! She wants to have a baby! Her own!'

"'Ah,' sighed the reverend, folding his fingers in meditation . . .'"

Reverend Winstead folded his fingers in meditation and read what he had wrought. He was not unmindful of the significance of this occasion and the attendant rituals: the locked door, the cleared desk, the filled pen, the new writing pad. It was a little like lying, he reflected, and trembled with the excitement of transgression.

It was on his thirtieth birthday, a few weeks ago, that he had walked downtown to see a movie but on the way had stopped in at the newsstand and, after glancing through a few magazines, had on impulse purchased a copy of *Writer's Digest*, because that issue contained an article entitled "Writing as a Second Career" by a well-known novelist who, in private life and under a different name, was, like Emory Winstead himself, a clergyman. The article had affected him more than anything he had read since stumbling upon Bonhoeffer in the original German during his last year at theological seminary.

If the truth be told, Emory Winstead was of late only nominally a clergyman, going through his round of duties with all the cold efficiency of a machine, discharging his obligations with an indifference concealed from everyone but his wife, Diana, who suggested that he take up rug braiding or chair caning as a hobby. Instead, he was taking up, as of this morning, the craft of fiction.

The article had advised him to begin at home in search of subject matter, and although none of his parishioners were very wealthy, and none, to his knowledge, had a daughter dying of leukemia, at least he could identify with the Reverend Norris and the unique moral burden that Arthur Manning was asking him to share.

His problem now was to give form to the minister's reply, beyond that awed "Ah" that the minister had sighed and that remained hovering on Emory's manuscript like a pesky and distracting fly. Was he right, he wondered, in keeping secret from his wife his literary ambitions? Mightn't it be better if he threshed out his plots in conversation with his wife?

A glance at his watch told him that he had been staring at his folded fingers for an unconscionable time. He took his empty coffee cup and returned with it to the kitchen, where Diana was preparing petits fours for an afternoon meeting of the Ladies' Aid. He refilled his cup but did not go back to his study at once. Instead, he sat down at the dinette, and after staring at his wife's back for a while, he spoke to her. "I had an unusual conversation on the phone a little while ago." It was so easy to lie, once one begins, he reflected.

"Yes?" said Diana, not turning from her work.

"One of our members—I can't tell you which one, because he swore me to secrecy—but one of our members is in a dilemma. His daughter has leukemia, and the doctors have given her only a year to live. He wants to do all he can to make her last year a pleasant one, and he is rather well-off, so he promised her she could have anything she wanted—kind of a last request, you see—and the girl decided—but get this: she's only fifteen years old—she decided she wants more than anything else to have a baby."

Diana turned around and looked at him. Her eyes narrowed as she stared sidelong at him and said, "I don't believe it."

He smarted at this accusation, but something in him—ambition, determination, pride—compelled him to raise three fingers and say, "Boy Scout's honor."

"But what are you saying?" demanded Diana. "A fifteen-year-old girl, dying of leukemia, wants to be a mother? She must be crazy! Does she have in mind any particular person who will father the child?"

"No," said Emory solemnly. "That is the problem."

"I just can't believe it. Who—" Diana paused, then asked hesitantly, "Is it that Henly girl, what's her name, Grace Henly?"

"No, it isn't Grace. I can't tell you."

Puzzled, Diana frowned and wiped her hands on her apron several times while thinking. Then she pointed a quick finger at her husband and said, "I know! It's Patricia Stedman, and I'll bet you anything that she's already pregnant, the way she runs around with that Tommy Ashford, and her father is just making up the whole story about her having leukemia so you will marry them!"

Emory shook his head and smiled. "No, it isn't Patricia either. I really can't tell you, but I'm convinced the father is telling the truth, and he wants me to tell him what he should do, because, after all, he did promise her that she could have anything she wants."

"It's incredible," Diana firmly announced and returned to her work but continued talking over her shoulder. "Because, in the first place, no fifteen-year-old girl in her right mind would want to bring a baby into the world if she knew the baby wouldn't have a mother for more than a few months. And in the second place, any fifteen-year-old girl whose father told her she could have anything she wanted would probably ask for some special present, like a trip to Hollywood or something, for goodness sake, but not—"

"Diana," said Emory, "all I'm asking you is: What should I do? What can I tell the girl's father?"

Diana did not answer. She busied herself with her pastries.

After a while, her husband grew impatient and said, "Well?"

Diana turned to face him again. "Em," she said gently, "is this all just some kind of parable that you're trying to work into your next sermon, and you want to try it out on me first?"

Genuinely taken aback, he said, "You don't believe me?"

"Frankly, no," she said and turned away once again.

"Ah, well," he said as he rose to leave the room, "I suppose I'll just have to wrestle with the problem all alone. All alone."

"Not all alone," she said. "Try it on God."

Shocked at his wife's blasphemy, he left the kitchen and returned to his study, where he sought in vain to resume work on the manuscript. Perhaps the plot actually was a bit farfetched. Perhaps he should endeavor to make use of materials for whose veracity his own experience could vouch. He considered the possibilities: a story about old Lockhart, venerable deacon, who on his deathbed had confessed to Emory a life of private sin . . . but sin that, unfortunately, was hardly printable, even by today's standards. Or then there was Mrs. McKay, who struggled with great odds and poverty to give herself an education after the death of her husband and finally earned a PhD in social work. An inspiring tale. But Karen Manning, with cancerous cells invading her lymph tissues and in her little heart a burning desire to fulfill the destiny that nature had intended for her, held a firm grip on Emory's imagination and will, and he knew that if he would write anything at all, he would write of her.

That night, in bed, he said aloud, as if talking to the ceiling, "I think I will tell him that if he can satisfy his own conscience that it is a noble thing to do, he should try to find a young man willing to offer his . . . his seed. God would not wink, nor look the other way, but gaze with fond tolerance on the scene." But Diana, he discovered, was already asleep.

Friday was visits day, to the county home, the jail, and elsewhere, and Saturday he worked the sidewalks of Main Street, distributing leaflets for the civil-rights organization to which he belonged. Then, of course, there was Sunday. So it was late Monday afternoon before he got back to his story and found that it had not jelled but chilled. As if he were deliberately packing dry ice into the project, he spent his time writing not the story but instead a list of questions: Assuming a young man could be found, would he become only a donor for artificial insemination, or might he be permitted to impregnate Karen in the customary fashion? Where would Karen go during the gestation period? Would there be any objection from her doctors to the whole scheme, perhaps out of fear that pregnancy would shorten her life still more? After Karen dies, what becomes of the baby? Placed for adoption or raised by Karen's parents? What if, before she died, medical science found a cure for leukemia? Is leukemia actually incurable at present? If not, what about hemophilia, lupus, or some other disease? What if Karen's mother or, indeed, her father himself should object to Reverend Norris's recommendation? What if Karen herself, in her innocence, did not understand the facts of life and did not comprehend the mechanics of sex or the rigors of pregnancy and childbirth? Wouldn't it be better if Karen were sixteen or even seventeen? Eighteen? Was it true, as his wife implied, that no girl, not even a strange, quiet, lovely, and lonely creature like Karen, would ever entertain any such wish?

His furious scribbling of this inquisition was interrupted by a knocking on his door, and he said, "Come in" before remembering that he had locked it. Unlocking and opening it, he thought at first that he was faced with Karen herself, but it was only Grace Henly, holding what seemed to be the tail end of some exotic bird.

"I've come to dust," said the child.

"Dust?" said Emory and then remembered that a committee of the Young People's League had volunteered (or been appointed by their economy-minded elders) to take over the janitorial chores of the church and parsonage.

"I could come back later if you don't want to be disturbed," said Grace, who was polite, fifteen or sixteen, but not nearly so pretty as his Karen.

"Oh, come on in," he said and stood aside. She walked into the room and immediately began to flick her duster over the bookcase. He returned to his desk, sat down, and found himself watching her. Soon, the sunlight that streamed in through the diamond-paned windows was saturated with floating particles of dust. Busily, Grace dusted everything and then turned to go, but he said, "Grace, could you spare a minute?"

"Sure, Dr. Winstead," she replied, but uneasily.

"Have a chair," he said, motioning her to sit down beside his desk, and she did. She crossed her legs, revealing a pair of gaudily patterned stockings, and lay the feather duster down atop his desk. "How's everything going?" he asked.

"Just fine," she said and began chewing a hangnail.

"Schoolwork and all?" he said.

"Okay," she said. "Just fine, I guess."

"Well, Grace—" he began, quite at a loss to formulate his request for the information that he desired from her. "I'm practically an old man, you know," he said lightly and chuckled, "and I can't always remember how the minds of young people are working these days. But perhaps you can help me. You're old enough now, Grace, to know—"

"I know what you're going to say," Grace broke in, nervously but indignantly, "and all I'm going to say is that it isn't true! If Patsy was the one who told you, then you know it's a big lie, because she's just jealous because Tommy took me to the movies Saturday night instead of her, and anyway, she wouldn't really know, because Tommy wouldn't have told her, and besides we were only—"

"Now, hold on a minute, Grace. Let's not—"

"Oh, I hate her!" Grace bawled, breaking into tears. "She thinks she's so pure and Christian. Why, I could tell you some of the things *she's* done, but you wouldn't believe it. And with Tommy too! I'm not any worse than they are! Why do you pick on me? After I've come all the way up here to dust your study for you . . ."

"Grace, Grace, Grace," said Emory and fetched a Kleenex from a box in his drawer and gave it to her.

She snatched the Kleenex from him, dabbed her eyes, sniffled, then gave her head a proud toss and said, "Okay, I'll admit it. It's true, but only because we didn't have any place else to go, and I just wanted to get even with her for being so stuck-up about it all the time. But I won't ever do it again, I promise, and please, please don't tell my mother. Oh, please don't let her know about it—"

He patted her shoulder and said, "Oh, I won't; I promise," and out of gratitude, she broke into tears again, and he gave her another Kleenex and patted her shoulder some more. He realized that whatever it was she was confessing had been confessed too far for him to wriggle out from under the assumed but mistaken role of accuser, so it was too late for him to explain otherwise, and he could only say, "But why did you do it?"

"Do you mean why did I just *do* it, or why did we do it in the church?"

"In the *church*?" he said but clipped off the question mark at the last instant.

"Because there wasn't any place else to go, and, well, it was Tommy's idea, not mine, and . . . and, well, it was just dark and convenient, that's all. But I know it was wrong, and I know God will punish me for it, won't He? And I'm going to pray for forgiveness every night for the rest of the year, and I swear on the Bible I won't even look at Tommy again, and Patsy can have him if she wants him, and they can both roast in hell! Oh,

I'm sorry! I didn't mean to say that, but if you only knew how bad both of them are, you would be ashamed that they go to your church." And Grace sobbed and sniffled for a while longer.

"There now," he said at last when she had gained some control over herself. He realized that she had maneuvered herself, under her own impetus, right into the place where he had wanted her in the beginning, so he took this opportunity to ask, "Would you like to have a baby?"

"Oh, don't worry about that," she said. "Tommy had a . . . he had a thing; you know, a *thing*. He showed it to me."

"That's not exactly what I meant," he said. "I mean that if you could, and it was okay with everybody, would you enjoy being a mother—I mean, having a baby?"

"Huh?" said Grace and stared at him.

"Do you like babies?" he asked.

"Oh, sure, but—"

"This has nothing to do with you. I mean it has nothing to do with this other business about you and Tommy. I'm simply asking out of curiosity. Just wondering. Now, suppose . . . suppose you found out that you were going to die in another year and you wanted to do whatever you could to make your last year on earth worthwhile. Would you like to have a baby?"

"Whose?" said Grace.

"Oh, I don't know, whoever appealed to you most."

"Not Tommy," said Grace.

"No. Just imagine anyone. Maybe your favorite movie star."

"Paul McCartney?" asked Grace, brightening.

"Anyone."

"Well, maybe. But we would have to get married first."

"Why?"

"*Why?* You don't think I would want to have a bas—an illegilable . . . an illetigimate child, do you?"

"But if you were going to die?"

"Why do I have to die?"

"Just suppose. Just imagine that's the way things were going to turn out. Would it be absolutely necessary that you be married to the father of your child?"

"Absolutely," Grace said with such firm conviction that he realized he would have to revise the present lines of his plot.

"I see," he said. "Well then, let me put the problem in a different form.

Suppose you were going to die in a year, and your father was very wealthy, and he told you you could have anything you want. What would you ask for?"

"Wow!" said Grace. "I would make a whole list of things."

"No. Suppose it could be just *one* thing."

Grace pondered the decision at some length and finally announced her choice: "A houseboat."

"A houseboat?"

"Yes, just like the one I saw in this movie one time. It had eight pretty rooms and a kitchen and everything, and you could even go across the ocean in it. I would get that boat and spend my last year just floating around all over the world."

"Ah," said Emory. "But you don't think that you might possibly want a baby."

"Not on a houseboat," Grace said. "My goodness. It would kill all the fun."

"I mean instead of a houseboat. Wouldn't you like to be a mother before you die?"

"Not particularly."

"Why not?"

"Well, gee, Dr. Winstead, you don't have any children yourself, so maybe you don't know what it's like. But when my brother was a baby, he was a real pest. Messy diapers all the time and all that crying, and he used to swallow things and have to go to the doctor. Who would want to spend their last year on earth taking care of a *baby*?"

"Well . . ." said Emory.

"Besides," said Grace, "just think about that poor baby, growing up with a dead mother—I mean growing up without any mother because the mother died and having nobody but the father, who has probably turned into a mean guy because he lost his wife because some people made him marry her because she was going to die . . ."

"I see," said Emory, and said nothing more.

"What a funny idea," Grace said reflectively after a while, and then she asked, looking at him strangely, "Why did you ask me?"

Emory shrugged, spread his hands, stammered, "I . . . I don't know. I . . ."

Grace waited uncomfortably for him to say something else, but he did not. He stared silently at his folded hands. Eventually, she said, "Well, I'd better go now. Remember what you promised, that you won't tell anybody, and I promise I won't ever do it again."

He nodded.

"Good-bye, Dr. Winstead. It was nice talking to you," she said. She waved and left.

She had forgotten her feather duster. He stared at it for a time. Eventually, it dawned on him that the feather duster was his own—that is, that it had come from the broom closet of the parsonage. He made a mental note to remember to return it now. He lifted it from the desk and took it out of his study and down the hall, but he forgot to stop at the broom closet. He carried the feather duster out of the house, across the lawn still crusted with old snow, and up the steps of the church. Carrying the feather duster upright as a crucifix, he strolled slowly into the empty church. The cavern of the interior reverberated with the sound of his footsteps. It was late afternoon, and the interior of the church was dark; he could only discern the shapes, the forms of the pews. *In my own church*, he thought, glancing around him and wondering which of the pews they had used. Or maybe the floor. Or the choir or even, God forbid, the pulpit. Young flesh. Lust in the bloom of youth that respects no place. Strange, because in the original outlines of his plot, he had envisioned something of that sort for Karen. If not actually the church itself, perhaps a room in the parsonage. But now Karen was dead to him. "Lord, I am not worthy," he said aloud, and listened to the acoustics of his church as they transformed his humble words into an actual prayer. To be not worthy to construct sound plots was bad enough, but to be not worthy to understand life was tantamount to being unsuited for the ministry. He had begun his project innocently enough as merely an avocation, a means of fulfilling hidden talent, a means of relieving the tedium of his career, yet now this well-meant enterprise had turned against him, destroying instead of relieving his career.

For a long time, he sat in one of his pews, although he was not aware that he was sitting there, thinking of the mysteries of youth, the chemistry of desire, the failure of intellect, and the brief, hard life-span of dreams. Supper was cold when his wife found him there, still clutching the feather duster, and before she got him out of there, he had managed to tell her about his lie, and to apologize for it, and to confess an old ambition to own and run a farm, and to ask her if she didn't think it was time they had some children.

Down in the Dumps

I T WAS THE WORST THING that could happen to him. Allegedly because he had borrowed without permission a small part of her pin money in a vain effort to recoup his losses at the harness track, his wife kicked Russell Thornhill out of the house—her house, her family homestead, not his. For a long time thereafter, he suspected that she had another reason; she was entertaining a lover, perhaps. He moved into a dismal apartment over Merton's Plumbing Shop, which was insufferably clamorous for twelve hours out of every twenty-four. He attempted to keep a watch on his wife's house, but the only way he could do this unde- tected was by lying in the wet grass in the empty field across the road. Probably as a direct result of his hours of lying there, he contracted pneu- monia and took to his bed for two weeks.

When at last he rose up, cured, from his sickbed, he discovered that his apartment was littered with trash and garbage. He packed it all into his little car—one the newspaper accident reports indiscriminately call "a foreign compact"—and hauled it away to the town dump.

Weekly dumping had been his regular chore during the five years he had kept himself in his wife's good graces, and he knew the dump by heart, including the man: the bearded, tanned, frostbitten, begrimed old man who lived in a ramshackle hut on the perimeter of the dump and kept the fires going and kept them contained and who subsisted, apparently, on whatever edibles and potables could be salvaged therefrom, including an abundance of minute dregs remaining in empty liquor bottles, which, taken together, constituted an immoderate weekly dose of alcohol. Russell Thornhill did not know the man's name and had never spoken to him beyond an exchange of observations on the afternoon's weather, but the man was as familiar as the dump itself.

The man always trotted out of his hut at the approach of a car or truck and then busied himself for the next ten or fifteen minutes, under pretext of recomposing the latest dumpings, in his never-ending search for a dram or two of booze. The sight of Russell Thornhill's foreign compact coming down the road always seemed to fill him with joy.

"No bottles this time," said Russell patronizingly as he began to heave his bags of refuse upon the burning pile.

"Bottles?" said the man innocently.

Russell did a pantomime of elbow bending. "Bottles. I've been sick for two weeks. No spirits. Doctor's orders."

The man shrugged, belched, and with his rake commenced to distribute Russell's garbage evenly amidst the flames.

The acrid stench of the blazing and smoldering mess, the cooking of decayed vegetables, the fumes of scorched tin cans, the boiling of juice-soggy ashes, assaulted Russell, hit him with the notion that there was something rotten elsewhere than in Denmark, that he was getting a dirty deal in this stinking life of his. Dumped me out like garbage, she did, he reflected, and thought that his eyes, which were smarting and running from the foul smoke that wafted into them, dripped with self-pity.

On the instant, he was possessed with an idea. A plan. A scheme. Supposing she had converted their once happy home into a den of iniquity, supposing she was receiving a lover or lovers into debased orgies, might not some evidence of it, in time, come to rest upon this sizzling heap? An excess of empty bottles, a surfeit of party snacks, a scribbled note, a billet-doux, a strange brand of cigarette butt, a man's cast-off or misplaced jockstrap . . .

"Say, fellow," he said, turning to the dump attendant, "how would you like to do me a little favor?"

The man regarded him with a noncommittal but attentive squint of the eyes. Russell then proceeded to outline his requirements: the man was to keep a sharp eye out for his wife's car, which was not a foreign compact but, indeed, a foreign behemoth, Spartanly squarish and rugged, with the spare tire mounted atop the hood, a green monster noted for its endurance on rugged trails and African safaris, and if and when it showed up and deposited its contents, the man was to carefully probe said contents in search of the aforementioned suspicious items or others that might tend to incriminate his wife.

The man listened patiently, then pursed his lips and looked skyward with an expression that suggested, to Russell, that he was waiting for legal tender to appear in the air.

Russell whipped out his wallet, withdrew a five, and tendered it to the man. "How's this?" he asked.

The man stared at the bill, and then, abruptly, without premeditation but with deadly accuracy, he expectorated a globule that hit Abe Lincoln square on the nose.

"Hey!" cried Russell.

"Filthy lucre!" said the man.

The two of them stood in silent confrontation for a very long moment while wisps of bitter smoke swirled and gathered around them like the funky vapors of hell.

Then Russell asked, "You won't do it?"

"Not for money," said the man.

"What, then?" asked Russell.

The man mimed Russell's previous pantomime of elbow bending and winked.

"Any preference?" asked Russell. "Scotch? Rye? Vodka?"

"So long as it's hundred proof," the man said, "I don't care if it's goat milk."

"Done," said Russell.

A few days later, he returned to the dump, this time, for the first time, without any garbage in his car but, instead, a fifth of Old Grand-Dad. The man met him at the door of his hut and invited him inside. Russell was reluctant to enter the hovel, but at least they would be insulated from the copious, odious smoke in there. Inside, he was given a chair, a patched-up straight chair obviously retrieved from dumpings, its cane or rush replaced by woven strips of inner tube, surprisingly comfortable. The interior of the shack seemed to be a four-sided montage of debris, the cream of the scourings: bright hubcaps, battered kitchen utensils, an armless doll, assorted radio parts that had been assembled into an operable instrument, articles of clothing, cans of foodstuffs without labels, and innumerable old magazines and paperbacks.

The man uncorked the offering of Old Grand-Dad. "Join me?" he invited.

"By all means," said Russell.

The man served up generous dollops in two unmatched tumblers of glass fogged with age, stain, and grime. He called Russell's attention to a jagged chip in the rim of his glass. "Watch you don't slice your lip on that."

Russell held his glass aloft. "Cheers," he said.

"*À votre santé*," said the man and drained off his glass in a single swallow, then exclaimed, "Aaahgg! Jumping mother of Jesus, it's great to gulp a big swill of stuff that's fresh and pure, no cigarettes in it, no peanuts, no soggy crumbs of potato chips, no coffee grounds! Ah, God!"

Russell smiled, happy, for his part, to have provided the uncommon nectar. Then, convivial, he said, "I haven't told you my name. I'm Russell Th—"

"Thornhill," the man said, breaking him off with a wave of his hand. "I know who you are. Thirty-two years old, married six years, no children, native of Sandusky, Ohio. Graduated from Harvard Law. Presently employed Palgrave, Trelawny, Horne and Osment, specializing in deeds, wills, and trusts. Given notice by L. Matthew Palgrave last November to 'shape up or ship out,' unquote. Average three fifths of bourbon a week, wife prefers scotch. Sometimes beer on Sundays. Lost eighty dollars on Shale Gleaner in the seventh at Hinsdale last month. Should've played Odd Job. Owe about three thousand to two different banks. Democrat, Unitarian, Community Chest, and Book-of-the-Month Club. TV dinners three nights a week. Prefer lamb chops. Use Nembutal, milk of magnesia, and vitamin B complex capsules. Much Bromo-Seltzer too. Also"—the man paused to pour himself another drink, a taller one this time—"also, your wife doesn't have a lover."

While Russell sat immobile with his jaw dropped wide open and his eyes vacant with stupefaction, the man rose and produced a large paper bag, which he upended, spilling its varied contents upon the floor. "*Regardez*," he said and prodded Russell.

There on the floor was an empty bottle of his wife's hand lotion. Also, an empty bottle of White Horse. An empty waxed box that had contained a frozen rock lobster tail. An empty carton of Tareytons, his wife's brand. A brassiere apparently scorched in the dryer. A pair of worn-out black panties. A few assorted wisps of blond hair plucked from a hairbrush.

Russell's eyes moistened at the nostalgic sight of these familiar items. Then he spotted a letter and opened it. It was from her mother. "Just leave the bastard alone," it concluded, "and one of these days, he'll come crawling home on his hands and knees, mark my words."

Some used Band-Aids, a worn-out toothbrush, an empty Kotex box, little else. "Is this all?" he asked the man.

"All that might be of interest," the man said. "The rest . . . grapefruit rinds, eggshells, banana peels, the usual crud."

Russell fondled the discarded panties, twisting them around in his hands. "How do you know so much about me?" he asked the man.

The man poured more whiskey for both of them. "You've been

dumping your garbage on me for something like five years, haven't you? Okay. I see things. I know more about what's going on in this town than anybody, but I haven't been out of this dump for ten years. Come on, I'll show you what I mean. Get your glass."

With his bottle and glass in hand, the man led Russell out of the hut and conducted him on a long guided tour of the dump. The brilliance of the sun, the liquid in his glass that seemed to keep refilling itself, the dizzying drifts of fetid smoke, the care with which he was required to pick his way through the rubbish, all conspired to stew him; before long, he had keeled over and out. It was dark night when he awakened, found himself lying beneath a blanket on the rough sagging bunk of the dumpman, who, he perceived in the gloom, was sitting nearby, reading a paperback by the light of an oil lamp, the empty Old Grand-Dad clutched in one hand, his face hardly recognizable for the steel-rimmed bifocals he was wearing. Russell lay still, requiring several minutes to orient himself; he remembered being shown things, being told to whom they had belonged or who had cast them off, being embarrassed too as, uninvited, he entered the private lives of the neighbors and townsmen, saw what they had discharged, scrapped, eliminated, sloughed off, the intimate and esoteric trifles of good people and bad and of good people who were really bad . . . Wow! The things a man could learn! *Pow!* Pow! The gunfire . . . he remembered the sharp cracking reports, and once, twice, the dumpman had yelled, "Duck!" and knocked him down into the dirt. Had the people, angry at the snooping, been firing at him? No. No, that hadn't been it. The dumpman had explained, talking in that same garrulous voice that had seemed to drone in his ear all afternoon, both gossipy and philosophical. What was it? Yes: aerosol cans. Aerosol cans, which, heated to a certain point in the flames, exploded their capsules and sent fragments of tin spraying out in every direction like shrapnel. "Lost a piece of my ear once," the dumpman had said and showed him the nick. All over the dump, aerosol cans—shaving cream, hair spray, whipped cream, window spray—going pow! pow! pow!

The dumpman turned his head and peered at him through the bifocals. Seeing that he was awake, the dumpman said, "Money is shit." Russell thought his voice sounded quite drunk. He raised himself up on one elbow. "Money is the diarrheal stool of a sick society," the dumpman went on, then asked a question. "Do you believe in Marx?" As if asking: Do you believe in God?

"No," said Russell. "When I was little, they told me he existed, but I never believed it." He chuckled. Then his head hurt, an awful hangover. Holy smoke, I got to get up and out of here, he said to himself. Back to civilization.

"Whiskey's all gone," said the dumpman, brandishing the empty bottle. Then he said, "No." He said, "No, I don't either. Never did. But he was right. When he said that money is all you get for working your ass off, and even then, the money you get isn't enough for the ass you worked off. The good part of the money goes to the rich, the bosses. The rest of us get the shit." He stood up. Remaining where he stood, tottering slightly, he jerked one foot out and kicked open the door of the hut and pointed, saying, "Look." Through the door, Russell saw white stars and red stars, the white stars up in the sky, the red stars the glow of burning ashes in the dump pile. "Look," said the dumpman again. "At least it ain't shit. *That* ain't, no. It's garbage. *Garbage*, Thornhill, and junk. Rubble. Some of it's organic, all right, but it didn't pass through the guts and bowels. It's all that's left over after everybody has used up the part that they paid their money for. Lots of it still usable. The poor folks, the farmers and the Negroes and the mill hands—what they leave behind ain't a bit of use. Can't cull it. Ain't worth winnowing. But the rest . . ."

The man stood in the door and began to yell out into the darkness, "Bring me your garbage, damn you! Bring it all and pile it on me! But leave your shit at home!"

Russell, standing now, nudged the man's elbow, said, "Excuse me," and edged his way past him and out through the door. "I'd better get on home," he said and staggered to his car and got into it.

"Bring another bottle, Thornhill!" the man yelled after him. "Any time!"

But Russell Thornhill did not bring another bottle, at least not for some time. What he did do first, a few evenings later, was to phone his wife and, contrite, groveling, meek, beg for another chance. "Take care of me," he asked. "I need you." She sighed and said okay.

Thereafter, he did, in point of fact, reform, giving up all of his vices except one, the bourbon, and even this he entrusted to his wife's discretion and regulation, giving her all of his monthly paycheck and letting her visit the liquor store as often or as seldom as she wished. Whenever he finished a bottle, he was careful to leave at least a jigger, if not two, remaining in the bottom, and on his weekly dumping trips, he would set the bottles aside on the ground, then quickly set fire to all of the rest of the trash and garbage and make a fast getaway before the dumpman could speak to him.

He found that he had lost interest in the races. Strictly speaking, he had lost interest completely in finance, economics, money matters in general. While this had obvious advantages, most notably that his wife was able to decrease their debts rapidly, it interfered with his work: he found it increasingly difficult to care about the prosperity of clients whose deeds, wills, and trusts were entrusted to his expertise. When a large manufacturing concern lost its lease as a result of his lack of care and interest, L. Matthew Palgrave called him in and said, "Two weeks, Thornhill. Severance pay for a month, but I want to see your desk empty in two weeks."

He communicated this news to his wife and asked for six dollars. She gave him the money without question, surprised that he had asked for some, the first time in weeks. He bought a bottle of whiskey and took it to the dumpman and asked, "What have you got on Matt Palgrave?"

"Palgrave?" said the dumpman, as he poured drinks for the two of them. "Your boss, huh? Never seen him."

"Doesn't he dump here?" Russell asked with desperation in his voice.

"You been avoiding me lately, Thornhill?" It was more an observation than a question.

"Busy," Russell said. "Terribly busy lately."

"Yeah. You been burning your trash like you were afraid to let me see it. What's the matter? Did I say something you don't like?"

"No, no. It's just that I—"

"You don't like me, do you?" asked the dumpman.

Russell said nothing. The man poured a larger drink for him and gestured for him to toss it off.

"You don't," said the dumpman. "I make you feel uncomfortable because I know so much about you. I know more about you than anybody, including yourself. Also, I'm dirty. I don't bathe but once a month, and I smell like garbage. Also, I talk bad. I'm just not in your class, right?"

"Look, let's not get into personalities, shall we? I came here because I've got to find some way of getting the goods on Matt Palgrave. Maybe you—"

"Why? Did he fire you?"

"As a matter of fact, yes, he did."

"Hah! So you want me to give you this bundle of love letters he's been getting from his mistress so you can blackmail him?"

"Do you have a bundle of love letters?"

"What if I did?"

"Listen, I'll *pay* you!" Russell beseeched, grabbing the man's shirt but realizing, abruptly, that money meant nothing to the fellow. The man was laughing at him. Russell released his shirt and said coldly, "I know a thing or two about you. I checked the town records. The town pays you forty-five dollars a month for keeping this dump. If you hate money so much, what do you do with that? Burn it? Eat it? Huh?"

"If you must know, I send it all to my boy. Every cent of it. He's got a little farm out in Oregon, and I'm helping him pay off the mortgage. Just another year and it'll be all paid up, and then I'm going to move out there and live with him and be a farmer. How about that? Ain't that nice?"

"Lovely," said Russell. "So if you'll accept a little donation from me, in return for something on Palgrave, then it will be that much sooner that you can go to Oregon."

"I never done anything dishonest in my life."

"You spied on my wife's garbage for me."

"The only thing dishonest about that was that I got a free bottle out of you under false pretense, when I already knew your wife never had no lovers."

"How about a case of whiskey? A whole case, man!"

"Nope."

"Aw, come on."

"Get thee behind me, Satan."

On, on into the night, Russell argued with him, to no avail, until he had consumed so much of the bottle himself that he no longer seriously cared whether he lost his job or not. The two men got high, finished the bottle, and the dumpman miraculously produced a new one from under the bed. Russell expressed delight and surprise, slapped the man on the back, and howled, "Y'ole reprobate, you!"

"Got that from a fellow came in here last week lookin' for his meerschaum pipe. Seems when his wife emptied the ashtrays, she wasn't watchin' what she was doin' and dumped out his pipe. Never did find the damn thing, but I spent a couple hours rakin' and pickin' around in piles trying to help him find it, and he gave me this bottle for my pains. Reminds me of one time a lady lost her Chihuahua doggy and come down here lookin' for him; she thought it might've got in the garbage by mistake . . ."

Russell and the dumpman passed a pleasant evening together, swapping anecdotes and philosophical speculations upon the degeneration of humanity, the vileness of cash, and the wastefulness of an affluent society.

Then they slept until noon the next day, Russell on the floor. For breakfast, the dumpman demonstrated how it is possible to reclaim coffee grounds and extract additional savor from them. After breakfast, they took turns with the dumpman's slingshot: Russell got the hang of the thing quickly and could hit a stationary bottle from ten yards, although he was no match for the dumpman, who could hit a thrown can twice before it landed and could knock off a rat or a woodchuck at thirty yards.

After his career had terminated at Palgrave, Trelawny, Horne and Osment, he spent more and more of his time with the dumpman. He felt a temperamental and ideological kinship with the man and even began to affect the man's dress, old corduroy trousers and a flannel shirt. Pooling their resources, they managed to remain together in a state of intoxicated bliss and jollity: Russell's outlook on his life became almost as carefree as that of his good friend. Of course, in time, the town began to gossip. Many people, taking their garbage to the dump, observed Russell there, noted the old clothes he wore, the stubble of beard on his jowls, and the same cast of grime upon his countenance as on the dumpman's. They thought it unseemly of one who had once been such a promising young lawyer, and they attributed it to alcohol, and their whisperings got back to his wife.

One evening, one of the increasingly rare evenings that he spent at home, as he was undressing for bed, his wife approached and began to spray him all over with a can of air freshener.

"Hey! Cut it out!" he protested.

"You smell like garbage," she said. "I don't want to sleep with you."

Another evening, she demanded, "Why don't you take a bath?"

And another, she asked, "When are you going to look for a job?"

"Quit pestering me!" he shouted.

His wife's nagging forced him to spend even more of his time at the dump. Even the dumpman himself became concerned and asked him one day about it. "Do you really like me so much?"

"You're my best pal," Russell said. "My only pal. This is the life for me."

But the idyll of their great friendship came to an end. Arriving at the dump one afternoon with a new bottle, Russell found his buddy lying facedown in the dirt, an ugly gaping wound in the back of his neck, flowing red.

Russell turned him over and cradled his body in his arms. He saw that the man was still breathing. "What happened?" he cried.

"Sons of bitches finally got me," the dumpman gasped. "Got me in the back."

"*Who?*" cried Russell.

"Them aerosol cans," the man whined. "Sons of bitches. Been popping at me for ten years. Always ducked. Not this time. No, sir. Got me in the back."

"Just hold yourself together, man, and I'll get you to the hospital."

"Too late. Too late. Send my boy a postcard."

Then the man died. A small item in the newspaper the next day called attention to the fact, giving the man's name and age, Kerwin Nairn, fifty-three (Russell was forced to realize that he had never known either), and suggesting that residents of the town should be more careful about leaving aerosol cans in their garbage. Also, the town manager wished to announce that there was now a vacancy for a "supervisor of town refuse yard," experience unnecessary, salary forty-five dollars a month. Russell applied. There being a paucity of applicants, he was accepted, with misgivings, by the town manager, who had been a friend of Russell's wife's family.

As for the wife, she moved to another town, subsequently sued for divorce, and attached a lien to Russell's small monthly salary. Russell moved into the hut at the dump, spruced it up a bit to suit his tastes, found an old envelope with the man's son's return address on it, and wrote a nice long letter of condolence. In his spare time, he hand-lettered neatly a very large sign that read, "Kerwin Nairn Memorial Refuse Yard," and then he built a gate on the dump road and erected this sign over the gate. It remained there for several weeks before the town officials called his attention to the fact that it was unauthorized and requested that he take it down. He refused. The matter was left to be decided at the next town meeting, where it died in committee.

Russell adjusted readily to his new life, and even the loneliness did not bother him, because sometimes, when he had accumulated a quart or so of mixed liquor leavings and treated himself to a binge, he would be joined by Kerwin Nairn, and the two old cronies would frolic late into the night, alternately cracking jokes at the expense of society and engaging in serious dialogues about existence, the meaning of honesty, the money-poisoned dying of civilization, and the transubstantiation or consubstantiation of Kerwin's body and blood with refuse. Taking Kerwin's advice, he was careful to search all garbage and extract all aerosol cans, and thus he lived a long, long time.

Telling Time

ONE TIME, THERE WAS A MAN in our town who could tell stories. Lion Judah Stapleton was his name, but everyone called him simply Lion Jude, or I thought they did, taking the nickname to refer not to his lionheart or to the emblematic lion of Judah (Genesis 49:9) but to one of his stories involving a mountain lion. Years later, I had gone away to college and was lying in bed one night, just lying there free-associating, as one does when one can't sleep, when the memory of Lion Jude came abruptly back to me, and I suddenly realized my error: his nickname had not been Lion but Lyin', because he told such stories.

But I decided to go on remembering him as Lion Jude. Not that I wasn't willing to accept the truth that all of his stories had been lies but because, as one does when one learns one's mistake, I preferred clinging to the original spelling and even endowing the memory of Jude with leonine qualities to go with it: he did, after all, possess a rather long, shaggy mane of hair; was muscular in the right places; and, when lounging, as he nearly always was, lounged with a catlike languor.

He was the only loafer on Ingledew's store porch who didn't whittle. Some said it was because he couldn't whittle and talk at the same time, but whittling didn't stop the other men from talking, not even Fent Bullen, who, alone among the whittlers, was actually carving something artistic. The other men just endlessly sliced their Barlows across sticks of cedar, basswood, or white oak, systematically covering their ankles with worthless shavings in the course of the day, but Fent Bullen employed a variety of fancy knives, some with spey blades and spear blades, to carve wooden chains, intricately linked, some links with a ball-in-cage or a slip joint, illusionistic, complicated, pleasant to the eye and fantastic to the finger. Nobody anywhere could compete with Fent in the carving of wood . . . but my story is about Lion Jude, not Fent. Nobody anywhere could compete with Lion Jude in the telling of stories. Or so we thought.

In fact—and this is a little story I sometimes tell on myself, in self-deprecation, because I was the only son of Stay More ever to attend college—until I was about nine or ten years old and had saved enough from my little earnings picking tomatoes to buy myself a Barlow and join the other whittlers on the store porch, I had the impression that a "store" is a place where "stories" are told! Oh, of course, I knew that the store sold things, and practically my earliest memory is giving Miss Lola Ingledew two pennies and receiving in return a large peppermint stick, but not long after that, I went out onto the store's porch and sat on the edge of it and listened to Lion Jude tell the one about the babes in the woods, which like to have scared me to death. It was a Saturday afternoon.

Years later, whenever I went to a movie on a Saturday afternoon, I remembered my first story at the store . . . and sometimes reflected, after a bad movie, that stories are much better than movies. Even today, when watching an occasional rented movie on my VCR, I prefer to play it on a Saturday afternoon. I guess I was seventeen or so and as grown up as I'd ever get when I heard the first truly bawdy tale from Lion Jude, the one about Cora and the Coke bottle, and realized it was a Thursday, not a Saturday, and discovered, much belatedly, that Lion Jude told his clean, wholesome, "fitten" stories, albeit however terrifying, on Saturday afternoons when younger people or children might be present, and on Thursdays, the store porch was reserved only for grown men, and not even Miss Lola Ingledew herself was welcome to go out onto her own store porch.

Didn't Lion Jude ever exhaust his repertoire? Oh, certainly, the regulars on the store porch had heard each one of Lion Jude's many, many stories more than once, but still, whenever one of them would say, "Tell us that'un, Jude, about that there preacher's wife and the Injun," Jude would rehash a familiar tale in such a way that his audience would roar with laughter, as if they'd never heard it many times before.

With a youth's misperception of anyone over thirty as "old," I thought that Lion Jude was an old man and thus well traveled and experienced with a long life from which he drew his tales. Actually, as someone once told me, Lion Jude had never traveled farther away from Stay More than the county seat, Jasper, a day's hike. He had a small, rocky farm somewhere on the yon side of Ingledew Mountain and a wife and children we never saw. But he was one of us: he had Stapleton kinfolks all over creation. When I researched his background for a college project, I learned that he was the grandson of the legendary Long Jack Stapleton, a Stay More minister famous for his ability to tell Bible stories so well that his audience could actually see and hear them.[1] Lion Jude wasn't *that* good, but he was proof that storytelling skill is hereditary.

He was poor, and it was known that Miss Lola Ingledew, the storekeeper, usually fed him at least his noon dinner and an occasional snack of Vienna sausages and crackers. And then, when Miss Latha Bourne bought out Bob Cluley's little mercantile store at the other end of Stay More's short main street and even succeeded in taking the post office away from Miss Lola's store, it was rumored that Miss Lola began to give Lion Jude a "salary," in the form of Day's Work chewing tobacco and occasionally a new pair of denim overalls or even a pair of shoes from the dusty and unfrequented clothing department behind the balcony on the second floor, in order to "keep" him at her store. It wasn't known whether she had expressly forbidden him ever to sit on the porch of Miss Latha's store, but whatever, he never went there, not even to check his mailbox. Probably, he never got any mail.

Thus, for a long time, the Ingledew store porch remained the primary gathering place for the men of Stay More and the theater for stories. In winter, they'd just go inside the store and sit around the stove, saving the best chair, the captain's chair, for Lion Jude. As far as I know, or can remember, Miss Latha's store didn't even have one of those big potbellied stoves with a smokestack ramming itself through the roof or a pickle barrel with a checkerboard mounted on it for the men who wanted to play games instead of, or in addition to, listening to Lion Jude's entertainments.

Now, it just so happens that there was a fellow sitting inconspicuously behind Miss Lola's stove in winter or at the least-traveled end of the porch in summer, places that I myself preferred and where I was thus sitting alongside him without knowing it, a fellow by the name of Henry Tongue. He was just one of the regulars, although there were two things irregular about him, or perhaps three if you consider that there weren't any other Tongues in Newton County: one thing was that he hardly ever spoke (which, at least for a few years until the jest grew stale, was the source of comments from the others about how possibly the cat had got Tongue's tongue), and the second thing, doubtless a result of the first, was that nothing was known about him, nothing at least worth remarking upon. It was not known what he did for a living; if, like nearly every other man, he had a farm, nobody knew where the farm was located or how large it was. He was neither rich nor poor. He was neither young nor old, thin

---

1. See *The Architecture of the Arkansas Ozarks* (1975), especially chapters 9–13.

nor stout, tall nor short. He was neither handsome nor ugly. His whittled shavings were the same size as everybody else's. If he had any identifying quality other than his taciturnity, it was his fondness for corn liquor: whenever the stoneware demijohn jug was circulated among the men on the store porch, he seemed to bob his Adam's apple a time or two more than the other swallowers. He probably did some further imbibing on his own, wherever he went, whenever he left the store, because he seemed to be in a kind of perpetual haze of intoxication, not sodden or even obfuscated but just piffled, tipsy, mizzled.

Nearly everybody called him Harry, not Henry, and I, just as I'd misunderstood "Lyin' Jude" to be "Lion Jude," misunderstood this as a teasing nickname, "Hairy," referring to the usual condition of his tongue, which was coated. Strangely enough, although Tongue's tongue was coated, he didn't have strong breath or bad breath, not that I can remember, but perhaps we just didn't notice it, because he rarely opened his mouth.

And when he finally did begin opening his mouth, in a big way, it was not at Miss Lola's store. It was at Miss Latha's. This was after she'd finally married her childhood sweetheart, Every Dill, and thus was no longer Miss Latha Bourne but Mrs. Every Dill, or simply Miz Latha, as everyone had to begin to call her. One Thursday afternoon, while Lion Jude was trying to add some new spice to a retelling of the one about the city girl's first encounter with a cow's teats, we noticed that Harry was missing. But one of us, by squinting his eyes and shading them against the sun, pointed across the quarter of a mile separating the two general stores and observed, "Yonder he sits." Sure enough, Harry was sitting on a nail keg (the most common store porch furniture) on the wooden porch that ran the full length of Miz Latha's storefront. He was not only sitting there; he was also talking and accompanying his words with gestures of his hands. He was not only talking, but he also had an audience of half a dozen folks, including Miz Latha herself. We waited, speechless; even Lion Jude was paused at the point where the city girl notices the cow has *four* of them. "Sonny," Frank Murrison said to me, "why don't ye mosey over thar and see what he's up to?"

So I went. I hung around Miz Latha's store only long enough to eavesdrop and be able to return to Miss Lola's store and report to the men there, "He's a-tellin some kind of a story."

"I God!" Lion Jude swore. "You don't mean to tell me!"

"Aint he got a nerve, though?" Fent Bullen said, but before long Fent, as well as Frank, Luther Chism, and myself, had all abandoned Miss

Lola's store porch in order to, we told ourselves, measure the audacity of the upstart Mr. Henry Tongue.

We had to report back that, indeed, the upstart was narrating stories and rather eloquently, in view of his years as a silent listener. Lion Jude was a mild man, never betraying any excitement except when he was feigning it in the acting out of some character's temper in one of his stories. But this situation, the fact that Harry had begun telling stories on Miz Latha's porch, made Lion Jude roar like a lion. Lion Jude angrily declared his suspicion that Harry had been sitting around silently all these years just to "gather up" Jude's stock of stories and now, having stolen Jude's material, was capitalizing on it. Probably Mrs. Latha Dill was paying him, maybe even cash money, maybe even . . . Lion Jude observed that Miz Latha, despite being such a sweet, lovely, proper, reserved lady, married now to the town's only auto mechanic, had been the subject of rumors for a long, long time before Every Dill came back into town and made an honest woman out of her. Nobody knew where she had been for the seven years she was missing from Stay More. Some folks had even suggested she might have lived in a large city supporting herself by prostitution. True or not, it was commonly known that before she disappeared, she had been confined for nearly three years at the state mental hospital, and many respectable citizens of Stay More still had reason to doubt her sanity. And it was commonly known now that the pretty little redhead, Sonora, who Latha had claimed for years was her niece, was actually her illegitimate daughter. Lion Jude wasn't going to come right out and accuse Miz Latha of *seducing* Harry, but it stood to reason, he said, that old Harry must be getting *something* out of it.

We were constrained to have to report back to Lion Jude that Harry was not actually stealing his material—that is, the stories he was telling were not stories he had heard from Lion Jude. All of Lion Jude's stories were tales as tall as the mountains surrounding Stay More, fabulations, fairy tales without fairies. His characters were nobody anybody had ever known. His events and episodes, whether ribald or chaste, were not only fictitious but farfetched; they entertained us by permitting us to experience vicariously things that could never possibly happen to us. They further delighted us by having happy endings.

Harry's stories, it was soon noticed, were taken from "reality," whatever that is. He may have been the only Tongue in Newton County, but somehow, he seemed to know the entire history of Newton and its neighboring counties and especially of Stay More. Harry could tell legends of the

Ingledew founders of Stay More, Jacob and Noah, that not even the living Ingledews themselves had ever heard, and he could take incidents that had just happened, or just been reported, and convert them into dramatic and often humorous narratives. When I was at the university, I took a course in folklore from Professor Mary Parler[2] and learned that such stories are called *memorates*: narratives of actual events, possibly events that the narrator himself has witnessed or experienced. I cannot find *memorate* in my unabridged dictionary, although I can find *märchen*, which is what Professor Parler said that Lyin' Jude's type of story is called. She was a quirky professor but an honest one. In fact, since part of the course assignment was to write a research term paper ideally based upon some aspect of one's own hometown, I wrote for Professor Parler a paper called "Telling Time" about the rivalry that developed between Stay More's two storytellers, Lyin' Jude Stapleton with his märchen and Harry Tongue with his memorates. (I might have earned a higher grade for the paper if I had not had the effrontery to include a footnote in which I observed parenthetically that my instructor's name, Parler, was the French infinitive of "talk," which is what both Tongue's name and his talent suggested. In her notes of criticism on my paper, Professor Parler did not comment on that; she did call my attention to the existence, in England, of a folklorist by the name of Ruth L. Tongue, who had written *Somerset Folklore*, *Further Somerset Folklore*, *The Chime Child, or Somerset Singers*, and a fine book that I now possess, *Forgotten Folk-Tales of the English Counties*. Miss Parler wryly speculated that my Henry Tongue might be a distant kinsman, at least by marriage, of this Ruth Lyndall Tongue.)[3]

---

2. Mary Celestia Parler (1904–81) was a professor of English and folklore at the University of Arkansas, a founder of the Arkansas Folklore Society, and the second wife of "the preeminent Ozark folklorist," Vance Randolph, one of Harington's very favorite writers and inspirations. (A fictionalized "Vance Randolph" narrates Harington's 1996 novel, *Butterfly Weed*.) "Mary Celestia Parler (1904–81)," CALS Encyclopedia of Arkansas, Central Arkansas Library System, last modified May 10, 2018, https://encyclopediaofarkansas.net/entries/mary-celestia-parler-3616/.
3. Ruth Lyndall Tongue (1898–1981) was a "real" but eccentric and apparently unreliable English folklorist whose every story (according to at least one scholar) forced readers to "filter through, trying to figure out what elements came from older folklore and what came from her imagination," even though (according to the same scholar) those very stories prove consistently "memorable, haunting, and usually a lot of fun," all of which lends credence to Parler's speculation about her likely kinship to Harington's Harry Tongue. "Ruth Tongue (1898–1981)," Writing in the Margins, https://writinginmargins.weebly.com/ruth-tongue.html.

But as far as Tongue's "payment" was concerned, Harry was not known to be receiving from Miz Latha even the "salary" that Lion Jude was getting from Miss Lola—that is, Harry was taking his noon dinner elsewhere before showing up at Miz Latha's in the afternoon, and if she was treating him to free snacks, soda pop, candy, or tobacco, nobody ever caught her at it. Since Tongue was pretty well lubricated when he told his stories, it was commonly believed that Miz Latha was keeping him well supplied with some of Luther Chism's best moonshine, Chism's Dew as it was known, but nobody ever saw her passing him a jug.

Why, then, did he betray Miss Lola Ingledew by taking business away from her store? For, indeed, not very long after Harry had begun to regale the porch sitters at Miz Latha's with his memorates, Miz Latha's business noticeably improved, and Miss Lola's noticeably declined. One by one, Lion Jude's congregation deserted him. In desperation, he himself, one memorable July afternoon, suddenly interrupted his account of the rich man's daughter and the beggar short of the climax and, thwarting his three listeners (although they knew how it turned out), stood up, hitched up his overalls, spat a larger than customary globule of half-masticated Day's Work, and ambled slowly up the dusty road toward Miz Latha's store.

The large crowd listening to Harry tell the story of the visit of Jesse James and his gang to the Stay More gristmill of Isaac Ingledew turned their heads away from the speaker to observe, almost sheepishly, the approach of the former unchallenged master of storytelling. Harry himself suspended the great James gang on their horses as they attempted to ride up to the mill porch and let his stilled tongue lie stunned in his mouth.[4]

Lion Jude spoke to Miz Latha, handing her a nickel. "Need me one a them sody pops." It was one of the things Miz Latha's store carried that Miss Lola's did not, since Miss Lola had never bothered with the expense of subscribing to the delivery of block ice for a soda pop cooler. Miz Latha took him into the store and let him pick his choice, a Grapette, from her cooler.

All of this was just a diversion so that nobody would pay much attention when Lion Jude slipped back out onto the porch and tried to hide

---

4. For Harington's full account of Jesse James's attempted invasion of Stay More, see the eighth chapter of *The Architecture of the Arkansas Ozarks*.

himself in the shade of the doorway, where he leaned up against the wall and drank his Grapette and listened while Harry went on with his story.

Now, there was another essential difference between Jude's stories and Harry's stories, apart from the one being fabulous and the other actual: it was a matter of style; Jude was a taker-outer, and Harry was a putter-inner. Any story by Jude always began simply, "One time . . ." never mind the fact it might have been the thirtieth time he was telling it. I always appreciated the ambiguity of the two words or their allusion not just to the long-ago, faraway, never-never *time* of the story but also to the fact that whatever plot he was narrating, whatever episode or imagined event, happened only *once*. It was unique; it would never, ever anywhere happen again.

A story by Harry, on the other hand, might begin with a variety of introductory phrases. He eschewed the customary "Once upon a time" as being not only trite but condescending to his audience. If the story he told was prompted by someone's mention of the person involved or the family involved, he might begin with "That puts me in mind of . . ." or "Speakin of ole So-and-So . . ." but more likely something like "Did ye know that many year ago it come to pass that . . . ?" or "Let me tell y'uns about the time that . . ."

If, for instance (hypothetically, of course), each of these storytellers were given the charge to tell a story about himself, Lion Jude would have begun, "One time, there was a feller who had a name for spinnin right wondrous yarns . . ." whereas Harry would have started out, "Now, it happened that there was dwellin in Stay More a certain ole boy who wasn't good for nothin, but come the shank of evenin around the porch of Miz Latha's store, he shore could charm the peepers down outen the trees with the masterest histories . . ."

Lion Jude listened carefully to Harry's resumption of one of these master histories, about the James gang, and then the one about the nearly incredible Battle of Whiteley's Mill, during the Civil War, in which Newton County soldiers on opposite sides fought each other for two hours with rifle and cannon without one single battle death occurring.[5] I watched Lion Jude out of the corner of my eye but could not quite imagine what he was thinking. His eyes were fixed into a squint of concentration to go with the furrow of his brow. I believed he was taking a lot of mental notes, especially about Harry's methods and style, if not his subject.

---

5. See the sixth chapter of *The Architecture of the Arkansas Ozarks.*

Surely he was studying Harry's delivery, so much in contrast to his own: Harry's inflections, his gestures, the changing tempos of his speech, even the postures of his body, were so different from Jude's. Harry's were more elaborate, more conspicuous, more a part of the story itself. Lion Jude remained there until the shank of the evening had become the thigh and everybody went home for supper.

But was Lion Jude inspired by his rival to switch to the telling of memorates? No, he was not, nor was he motivated to emulate Harry's more convoluted and embellished style, nor to mimic any aspect of his delivery. To the contrary on all three accounts, he began to tell, to his diminished audience at Miss Lola's store, stories of increasing make-believe, implausibility, and unnaturalness. His delivery, already inflectionless and nongestural, became almost invisible. And his style became more spare and terse, even to the point of what modern literary critics have called minimalism. For example, one of his favorite risqué anecdotes, involving a man and a woman in a hotel room playing a drunken game of rushing naked at each other from opposite sides of the room to meet in congress in the middle, had required perhaps five minutes to tell in his original version of it but was now reduced to less than sixty seconds of clipped short words foreshadowing the punch line, "Everbody's upstairs a-watchin the doctor try to git some woman off a doorknob." It was hard to believe that any of the incidents in Lion Jude's stories were actually capable of happening.

Strangely enough, but fortunately, as far as I was concerned, Lion Jude began to win back some of his lost audience. Since I personally preferred him, I was one of the first to return to Miss Lola's store, and thereafter, I "rooted" silently for Lion Jude to win the contest between the two storytellers. In my paper for Professor Parler, I attempted to analyze the reasons why Lion Jude eventually won the contest, and while Professor Parler challenged my arguments with many red-penciled notes in the margins, I think I was correct in observing some essential differences between the two—not simply that Lion Jude was always sober while Harry was drunk (which would seem paradoxically to contradict the basic nature of their stories, Harry's being soberly factual and real, Lion Jude's being intoxicatedly farfetched and fantastic), but more importantly that so many of Harry's stories had tragic endings while Lion Jude's had happy endings.

If a story had to end, people felt, perhaps knowing that Stay More itself was ending, it ought to end with a smile on its face. A story ought to end, if not with some revelation that leaves you feeling good (and I am saving a revelation for the end of *this* story), at least with some hope for oneself. Lion Jude's stories were optimistic; Harry's were pessimistic. That's what it boils down to.

Whether or not Lion Jude "won" the contest, the restoration of Lion Jude's congregation was actually more exciting than the actual numbers of listeners might have indicated, because Stay More was dying, and the people disappearing from either Miss Lola's porch or Miz Latha's porch were not doing so in favor of the rival storyteller but because they were leaving to go to California or to some larger town in Arkansas, Jasper or Harrison or Little Rock, or simply to die. Whatever, they were not staying more.

Miss Lola was wrong to blame Harry for the decline and death of the old Ingledew Store. Her store closed and was boarded up not because of the competition from Miz Latha's store but because of the competition from all the fancy stores in California and from something new in Jasper called a "supermarket." Miz Latha's own store would not last much longer before it too was shut down.

In fact, if we consider the victor to be the last one left in the field, Harry was already gone before Lion Jude told his last story to the crew of workmen whose job was to nail up boards over the doors and windows of Miss Lola's store. My research for Professor Parler's project was not successful in tracking down Tongue's ultimate whereabouts. He was known to have lived in Jasper for a while after leaving Stay More and to have told a lot of stories there. He later moved to Harrison, the largest town in that part of the Ozarks, and there is a photograph of him holding forth to a large crowd of whittlers and loafers on the steps of the Boone County Courthouse. There is an item from the *Arkansas Democrat* that names him as the second prize winner in a state storytelling contest and gives his residence as Little Rock. Where he went from there, nobody seems to know, although one informant related that he had moved to a larger city, Memphis or New Orleans.

Now it seems to me that Tongue lost the Stay More competition for one simple reason (and Miss Parler's red handwriting at the end of my paper says, "Perhaps you are right"): although he told memorates, although everything in his stories supposedly had actually happened, although his stories were so "real" that like life itself they did not end pleasantly, he could not avoid converting all of his "ordinary" people into heroes and heroines, and thus making them extraordinary, and thus making us, hapless listeners, feel inferior to them.

To really love a story, we have to lie to ourselves, and the biggest lie we tell is a telling to time: that the *one* time of the story is our time, is *now*, for the life of the story, for the life of our listening to it, being in it. Harry Tongue took people and events and elevated them to some pantheon where we could only admire but never *be* them. And all his people died, and all his events ceased happening, and his time was *told*, and old, and gone.

Not so long ago, I drove back to Stay More for the first time in many years. My parents no longer live there; I have no relatives living there. The town was abandoned except for some bum living alone in the old Ingledew place that had briefly been a hotel. I didn't speak with him. Miz Latha was still living on the outskirts of town, and I visited with her a little and mentioned the paper I had written for the folklore class. She smiled and told me that Jude Stapleton was still alive. She occasionally spotted him along the banks of Banty Creek or in her orchard meadow. Since he was always talking, she assumed that he was just talking to himself, as old people sometimes do ("As I often do," she confessed). She never spoke with him; she hadn't spoken with him since he'd bought that bottle of Grapette from her so many years ago. But she'd discovered that he usually had some kind of audience in the form of birds or an occasional rabbit or squirrel or even insects. "You've heard of 'tellin the bees'?" Miz Latha asked me, and when I nodded, she said, "Well, he's tellin his stories to bugs."

I searched for him that day but couldn't find him. I knew he was there; I know he is still there yet. Harry Tongue made Stay More into a mythical place that belongs in books on shelves; Lion Jude Stapleton keeps the time of Stay More and tells the time to stay more, tells the time to be *one* time.

The Freehand Heart

I

On an old sycamore tree near the village of Stay More is a triteness that ought to be explained. Where the bark has peeled to expose the whitish inner bark, several persons at different times have carved their initials into the wood, but one person has attempted a heart surrounding a pair of initials. It is not possible to date any of these carvings.

The initials of the girl, who was never there to see them carved, are "O. K.," and the initials of the carver are . . . but let us assume the letters are "R. R.," and let us just say that the name of the carver was Richard Roe. Dick met Meg in the ninth grade, in a city two hundred miles from this sycamore tree. Even her teachers assumed that *Meg* was short for Margaret, but they were wrong. And her last name . . . Oh, the only reason Dick was drawn to Meg in the first place, the only reason he became the only one of all her classmates who would even pass the time of day with her, let alone, as he eventually did, actually *befriend* her, was his fellow feeling, sharing with her the embarrassment: ever since the first grade, they had made fun of his name, Dick, long before he even understood what a dick is, and now, in the ninth grade, he had belatedly encountered the word *cunt* only recently, and here was this new girl, an outsider from faraway Chicago, talking funny, with a hideous last name, Koontz, which all of us had a whole lot of fun mispronouncing.

The Latin teacher, Miss Harris, called the roll each day, and now, well into October and the semester half over, Miss Harris stared over the tops of her bifocals at the strange face sitting in the seat in front of Dick's and said, "It seems we have somebody new. Margaret Koontz. Are you just starting? Will you have problems catching up with us? Do you know how to say *daddy* in Latin?"

The new girl did not know that we remain seated while answering the teacher. She stood up. Not only did she stand, but she had a very erect carriage, almost a military bearing, which, from the beginning, gave everyone the notion that she was awfully proud of herself. "My name is Meg, not Margaret," she said. "Meg Koontz." Dick was destined never to forget the way her lips formed her last name, making a cute little pucker, or the sound, a little grunt of gladness. "Yes, I have just moved here from Chicago, but I had already started taking Latin at Woodrow Junior High there, and I hope I don't have any problems. *Tata.*" She sat down.

All of us were amazed at the way she pronounced *I* as one crisp, clear monosyllable in the Yankee fashion, rhyming with *high*, but we scarcely had time to exchange sneering glances with one another before our mouths dropped open at her daring, dismissive terminal utterance.

Miss Harris was affronted. "'Ta ta'?" she said. "I hope you aren't going to get smart-alecky with me, young lady."

Meg Koontz stood again. "Ma'am? You asked me how to say *daddy* in Latin."

"*Daddy* is *pater* in Latin," Miss Harris said.

"Begging your pardon, ma'am, *pater* is *father* in Latin," Meg Koontz said. "A Roman kid who wanted to address his father familiarly, the way we say 'Pop' or 'Daddy,' would say '*Tata.*'"

"Oh?" said Miss Harris. Then she said it again without the question mark. "Oh. You may sit down, Margaret."

"Meg," she said. "My name is Omega."

"Like the wristwatch," Miss Harris said.

"Like the end," said Meg. "The last. Or like the subatomic particle in the baryon family with a mass three thousand two hundred seventy-six times that of the electron and—"

"Sit *down*, Miss Koontz," Miss Harris said.

"Whew shit," Bobby Hamill whispered to Dick, and at lunch in the cafeteria, Bobby gave a riotous impression of Meg that was almost audible to its subject, who sat alone at an empty table some distance away. Dick watched her. She did not seem to notice Bobby's lampoon. Late in the meal, she had a crumb of baked bean clinging to her chin, and Dick wanted to go wipe it off, but to do so, he would have to introduce himself and make some kind of small talk, and he wasn't ready for that.

There really ought to have been a better person than Dick Roe to have taken an interest in Meg Koontz. She needed someone more her equal in terms of looks, intelligence, or behavior. In terms of looks, Dick Roe was as ordinary as if his name had been John Smith. Meg Koontz, despite her awful name, was almost pretty: she was taller than Dick Roe (although he would soon catch up, and before the next summer was over, he would be taller than she), and she was almost fully developed in the right feminine places, although her undertow still had a trace of baby fat. Her brown hair was kept as neat and clean (he could smell it from where he sat) as the clothes she wore, and her brown eyes were not conceited but open, trusting, inquisitive, as if she really intended to withhold judgment until she had all the facts. In short, Meg Koontz was, on the surface, at least, cute and sweet and nice and even desirable, although Dick had just begun to associate desire with his family coevals, and he would not even have sexual dreams of Meg until the next summer, when suddenly, one night, she would surface and wriggle her nude body against his in such a way that he had a nocturnal emission.

And in contrast to her exceptional mentality, Dick was so stupid that he did not realize the risk he was taking when he befriended her and thereby became just as much an outcast as she, tainted with her superiority and otherness. "Hi," he finally wrote, the second month after her coming, and slipped it to her when Bobby wasn't looking, "My name is Dick Roe, and I'm sitting right behind you. But don't look now. Ha ha. I am having a lot of trouble with diclension (sp.) of all these verbs, and I wonder if you could help me out after school sometime."

He did not have to wait long to see her agile, delicate hand slipping behind her back with a folded reply. "This must be Wednesday," she wrote. "On Wednesdays, you have sausage for breakfast. Yes, if I can help you, I will. But declension is the inflection of nouns. The inflection of verbs is conjugation. I'll be glad to conjugate with you. Where?"

Dick studied this note. Years later, the double-entendre of "conjugate" would finally catch up with him and kick him in the butt, but now he was less embarrassed by his mistake in confusing declension with conjugation than he was by the thought she could smell his breath and tell what he'd had for breakfast. There was something about the *tone* of the note that was intimidating to him. Would he actually be able to speak to her, ever? More importantly, did he want to be seen speaking to her? Nobody else spoke to her. There was only one other Jew in the school, Ruth Goldfarb, and not many kids spoke to her, but at least she had been born in this town and talked like everybody else and was not totally ostracized, as Meg was. Dick carefully examined his motives: Did he really want Meg's help with Latin? He was going to flunk it one way or the other. There was no way he could ever memorize how *audio*, hear, gets changed into indicative active, present imperative active, indicative passive, subjunctive active, and all those pluperfects and participles, et cetera. No, the only reason he had passed that note to her was because he felt sorry for her. Just as he felt like a lost, friendless stranger in the world of ancient Rome, she must feel like a lost, friendless stranger in this little city so far from Chicago. "Can you stay after school, after everybody has gone, and just meet me here?" he wrote back to her.

II

Thus, for almost three weeks, until they were caught by Miss Harris, who made a well-meaning but embarrassing example of them, Dick met Meg in the Latin classroom when the rest of us were gone home. They sat not at their customary desks, one behind the other, but at Miss Harris's desk with the roles reversed: pupil Dick sat in Miss Harris's chair; teacher Meg sat in the chair beside it. She was not pedantic. She turned the learning of conjugations into a game that Miss Harris ought to have tried, and she did it without ever talking down to him or making him feel as stupid as he really was. He might almost have learned how to conjugate if he had paid closer attention or practiced at home, but he was distracted by the inescapable thought that this was really the first time he had ever been alone with a female, and he could not prevent his attention from wandering to such things as the way she talked, the unusual Yankee pronunciation of so many words, and the blouses she wore, always white, never the same one twice, as far as he could tell, and occasionally revealing the shape of the straps of her bra. Sometimes, while attempting to watch the way her lips formed *amo, amare, amavi, amatum,* he would take note of the pale lipstick she wore, and by the time she got into *amabamus, amabatis, amabant,* he would be lost in a daydream of giving her a kiss. Dick had never kissed a girl.

Their first two meetings were strictly business, on the subject of verb conjugation; their third meeting, they permitted themselves to exchange opinions of Miss Harris and of selected classmates; by their fourth meeting, they were beginning to tell each other about themselves. She was not a Jew, after all! "My father, if anything, is a Christian Scientist," she said. "Me, I'm nothing." The name Koontz, he learned, was originally Germanic, although not even her grandfather had ever been to Germany. It probably derived from *Kunst* ("despite the transposition of the terminal consonants," she said), which means art. All that Dick could think to say about that was to mention that he had a country cousin named Art Roe, short for Artis. His own patronymic was not remarkable except for the fact that another distant cousin, Elroy "Preacher" Roe, had been a Hall of Fame baseball pitcher. Did Meg like baseball? Not particularly, she admitted. He didn't either, very much, he confessed. And they discovered, even if in a negative sense, the first of many things they had in common.

One day, she asked him, "Why do they call you 'Jeth'?" He blushed and attempted to explain the teasing nickname, part of Jethro. Did she know the hillbilly character Jethro? Well, each summer, Dick's parents sent him to live with his grandmother, two hundred miles away, up in the Ozark Mountains, where most people still talked in the old-fashioned, lilting, easygoing way of so-called hillbillies. Dick loved to spend his summers there ("Remind me to tell you about the place," he told Meg), but the way people talked there was so infectious that when he got back home, it took him a month or two to get back to his old way of talking, and the other kids made fun of it ("Like they make fun of you") and had nicknamed him Jeth Roe because of it.

"Do they make fun of my talk?" she asked. "Is that why they don't like me?"

Dick had often asked himself why Meg was so unpopular. Of the four possible reasons—her strange name, her presumed Jewishness, her superior intelligence, and her Chicago voice—he had concluded that the latter was most likely the reason. But he wasn't sure. "Were you popular in Chicago?" he asked her.

"Not especially," she said. "But at least I had a girlfriend. And I miss her." Meg Koontz's eyes became a little watery, but Dick was glad that she had enough control not to let a teardrop roll out.

"If I was a girl," he declared, "I'd be mighty proud to be your friend." It was his first expression of feelings to her, and the words were out before he realized how fraught with sentiment they were, and he blushed.

"You don't have to be a girl," she told him, and reached out across the desk to where his hand lay on the Latin book and dropped her hand on top of his.

It was at that moment that Miss Harris came back into her room. "Did I leave my grade book?" she asked, as if it were a question either of them were capable of answering. Meg had quickly removed her hand from the top of Dick's hand, and they both had their Latin texts open in front of them, so it was convincing to explain to Miss Harris, as Dick attempted to do, that Meg was helping Dick learn how to conjugate. Miss Harris said that was splendid, but she'd prefer that they not do it at her desk. The next day in class, Miss Harris jumped on all of us for being so slow to learn the differences among genitive, dative, accusative, and ablative, and then she said, "Meg Koontz and Dick Roe have been staying after school all on their own to help each other with their verbs, and it wouldn't hurt if more of you did that."

"Whew shit, Jeth," Bobby Hamill whispered to Dick and flapped his hand loose at the wrist. At lunch in the cafeteria, Bobby said, "Hey, Jeth, how come you don't eat with her too?" and pointed to the table where Meg sat alone.

Years later, Richard Roe would often remember that moment and wonder if his life would have been any different if he had not done what he did: he picked up his tray and carried it over to Meg's table and sat down. Her great smile was more of delight than surprise. "You don't have to do this," she said.

"I don't have to be a girl either," he said.

III

Oddly enough, although we exhausted the possibilities of making jokes about dicks and cunts, country hicks and big city chicks, geeks and boneheads, or peas in a pod (our favorite was "nerds of a feather"), we all felt secretly relieved that one of us had done something to get acquainted with poor Meg Koontz. Despite our ridicule of him, Dick Roe was our covert hero, and while we were no longer allowed to speak to him in any but a taunting manner, we silently wished him well in his association with her, and we may even have been envious when we heard that the two of them had been seen together riding their bikes to a Saturday matinee.

Still, we watched for any opportunity to justify their exclusion, and once, when Meg emerged from the girls' room with a length of toilet paper clinging to her shoe and came into the cafeteria line unaware of it, we thought this was so ridiculous that Bobby Hamill got some Scotch tape and deliberately attached a long section of toilet paper to his own shoe and pranced around with it, until Dick ripped it off, wadded it up, and threw it into Bobby's face, which precipitated a fistfight that Dick lost.

Thereafter, since we were required to continue shunning or funning both Dick and Meg, lest we ourselves become the butt of jokes, we pretty much left them to their own devices and took for granted that they eventually became inseparable. Here again, we secretly envied them: the boys among us reflected how convenient it must be to have a girl you never had to ask for dates, because wherever you went, she did too; the girls among us wondered what it must be like not to have to sit beside the phone waiting for a boy to call. Any telephoning that Dick and Meg did was only to each other and was constant.

Boys and girls alike, we imagined that such an inseparable pair might possibly be doing, or trying to learn how to do, what male and female are built for and intended for. Although we made jokes about dicks and cunts, we were virgins, most of us, and we could only fantasize about what was happening occasionally or frequently during the long hours Dick and Meg spent together. Nobody knew where Meg lived, and we had only a vague idea of Dick's address, but we could easily picture some bedroom somewhere sometime when the parents were out and their bodies doing things together or trying, at least.

Dick's address, as it happened, was just a few blocks from the junior high school, but he never thought to invite Meg there, even to meet his parents. Meg lived at the opposite end of the junior high's district, in an old part of town, in a house from the previous century, too large for just the two of them, her and her father, who was the manager of a company that made lighting fixtures. Dick did not know, until the first time Meg invited him to the empty house, that she had no mother, or, rather, that her mother still lived in Chicago, and Meg never saw her anymore. Thus, because her father usually worked late, an hour or more past quitting time, they had the big house to themselves any afternoon after school, and that was where Meg continued trying to teach dumb Dick how to conjugate. Looking back from years later with great fondness toward all the hours he had spent in that house, Dick regretted that his inexperience, his stupidity, his timidity, his innocence, his whatever, had prevented him from even trying to turn verbal conjugation into physical. Often, he replayed those afternoons in his memory and tried to alter them so he could say the right thing, do the right thing, make the move that would have given them a chance to have sex.

They had both graduated from junior high before their first kiss. The last issue of the school's journal (there was no yearbook) had our graduation photographs with, under each, our "ambition" and "never seen without." Most of us were never seen without our tennis shoes or our freckles or sunglasses or a Hershey bar or a T-shirt or a readmission slip or our dad's Jeep, but Meg was never seen without Dick, and vice versa, although, under "ambition," it just said that Meg wanted to be a teacher and Dick wanted to own a farm.

The week after graduation, Dick was scheduled to take a bus to the town in the Ozarks where he would transfer to the mail truck that would, after many stops, get him to his grandmother's house. Meg and Dick spent much time talking about this. They seriously discussed the possibility that Meg might go with him. Dick's mother phoned the grandmother, who said she'd be just tickled to pieces to have Dickie bring his sweetheart with him, and she'd sure keep a sharp eye on the youngsters to make sure they didn't get into no mischief.

So all they had to do was get permission from Meg's father, Tata she called him. Tata liked Dick but had told Meg that he hoped she wasn't becoming too attached to her friend. Her father had already, in an effort to keep them from spending all their time together, arranged for her to take piano lessons five afternoons a week throughout the spring semester and into the summer, but that had still left them Saturdays and Sundays together, and they had biked together and hiked together all over town and even out into the country, and had had picnics together, and had gone to movies together, and had played cribbage together and even chess. And told each other everything, everything that ever crossed their minds (except, of course, their innermost feelings about their sexuality). Dick had told Meg all about the Ozarks and the little village his grandmother lived in and all the interesting and fun things there were to do there, and Meg was just as eager to get there as he was.

Tata listened gravely to her request. She assured him that she would have her own room in the grandmother's large house, and since the grandmother was home all day and all night long, Dick and Meg would be "chaperoned" more closely than they had been in Meg's own house. Meg told Tata that she would be despondent, just absolutely devastated, if she were separated all summer from Dick. Her father asked for a couple of days to think about it, and then he told her that he thought it would be better if she waited a year. If, after another year, her first year of high school, she and Dick were still such good friends, then she might go to his grandmother's with him. As a consolation, Tata offered to send her to Lake Sylvia, the Girl Scout camp, for the summer. But she burst into tears and told him she didn't give a damn about Girl Scouts.

When Meg reported her father's decision to Dick, they hugged each other in their disappointment, and then they talked seriously of running away together but decided that would bring them nothing but grief. Finally, Dick told Meg that he could, if she wanted, take a job as a bag boy at the supermarket and stay in town. His parents wouldn't like the idea, having grown accustomed to getting him out of their house and their hair for the duration of each summer, but they wouldn't force him to go. "Listen, Meg," Dick said to her, "just say the word; just tell me if you don't want me to go, and I won't."

"No," she said. "I know how much it means to you. I can't stop you. I don't want to try to stop you."

She rode in his parents' car when they took him to the bus station, and while they were waiting for the bus to be boarded, she took his hand and drew him between two adjacent buses, a narrow space, secluded, and said to him, "It's time, I guess, that we try to see if we can't kiss." And they could. Dick would never forget how that touching of their lips transferred to his heart, making it jump and fibrillate, for a moment scary. Then she turned and walked away and would not watch his bus disappear, as if she could not bear the disappearance. He had told her, in the course of telling her so many things about the country folk, of the Ozark custom, or superstition, that you should never watch anyone who is leaving go out of sight.

IV

They had agreed to write to each other, and they did. They spent every free moment composing letters to each other. She was so much better at words than he was, but he didn't let his sense of inferiority stop him from trying to tell her everything that he was doing, and while he could never speak of something like "love," whatever that was, he could constantly remind her that everywhere he went, everything he did, he pretended that she was with him. In his very first letter, he told her that he had been working hard, picking beans for the canning factory, and it was backbreaking work, but because he had pretended she was with him, working alongside him, he was kept from being worn to a frazzle. In her first letter, she told him that she couldn't stand being alone in her big house without him, so she had started going each day to the public library. She was writing to him from the library's music room, where she was listening to Rachmaninoff and trying to read Ovid's *Metamorphoses* in the original Latin. It was a nice room, with prints of cubist paintings on the wall, and usually she had the room all to herself . . . and to him: she too was pretending that he was with her, and sometimes she read the Ovid aloud to him. Actually, Dick had flunked Latin despite all the help she'd given him, and he couldn't imagine being able to understand what she was reading to him, but since they were just pretending, he pretended that he understood every word she spoke. He told her that he didn't have

time to read anything, which was just as well, because there wasn't anything to read at his grandmother's except the local newspaper, the *Newton
County Times.*

Before very long, however, he realized that there were some events in
his life that could not be shared with her, even in pretense. Each day after
picking beans, he and the other boys would go down to the creek for a
skinny-dip, to wash off the dirt and sweat and chiggers. He couldn't allow
Meg to be there in their presence, let alone for her to strip naked and join
them. He tried to make a joke of this in his letter to her, to explain why she
wasn't allowed to skinny-dip even in his imagination. She replied, "But
couldn't you pretend that you and I went somewhere farther up the creek
and skinny-dipped by ourselves?" The idea of this, the image of this, and
possibly his pretense that he actually did do it (the other boys may have
wondered why he was lost in thought) were likely responsible for the wet
dream he had that night, wet in more ways than one.

He couldn't write to her about that, although he considered it. Nor
could he write to her that the next day when the boys were fooling around
buck naked on the creek bank, they decided to have a little contest to see
who could get a hard-on quickest, and he, just remembering the dream
of the night before, won it. It was the first time he had ever won any kind
of contest, and he wanted to tell Meg about it just because he was proud
and also to let her know that it was her remembered nude image that
helped him win it. He even wrote it out on a couple of sheets of paper, as
discreetly as he could, but tore them up.

For her part, she seemed to be having difficulty revealing all the intimate details of the lives she was living, which were the lives of Ariadne
with Theseus, Medea with Jason, Thisbe with Pyramus, Daphne with
Phoebus, as told to her by Ovid, and which she tried to retell to Dick, but
haltingly with the details of the "relations" between the various couples.
"I have to 'hang up' now," she wrote. "It gets really salacious in this part,
and besides, my privacy has been invaded by some guy who comes into
the music room when I'm using it."

His grandmother did not even have a dictionary in the house, so he
couldn't look up *salacious.* Nor could he subsequently tell Meg of an
actual experience that was salacious: one time, the boys decided not only
to have a hard-on contest but also a jacking-off contest. Thinking of Meg
during it, Dick almost won but was narrowly defeated by his cousin Art
Roe. Dick told himself that if he had won, he might have had a reason to
write Meg about it.

Meg was obliged to report that she had struck up a conversation with the guy who sometimes came into the music room. His name was Peter, and he was a music major at the university, and he played some records by Debussy and Fauré that were new to her and that she liked. Dick didn't like the idea of Meg talking to some old boy, and he told her so, and while he was at it, he mentioned April.

The boys talked and joked a lot about a certain girl named April Swain, who lived at the next house up the road from Art Roe. Art claimed to have got onto a bed with her when the two of them were only ten years old and many times since, and all the other boys claimed to have gone into the bushes with her at least once. Dick first heard of her during the jacking-off contest, when all of the boys yelled, "APRIL!" at the moment of ejaculation. Dick didn't reveal this detail to Meg, but he did write to her, "If you don't quit talking to that Peter guy, I think I'll start chasing April." He was only half teasing, of course, and later regretted trying to make Meg feel jealous. But after all, maybe she had been trying to make him feel jealous by telling him about Peter. By coincidence, the same day he mailed that letter, his cousin Art said to him, "Come go home with me, Dickie, and I'll fix ye up with ole Aprilly." Dick was astonished to find that April was not just some feisty country piece but a very pretty girl, very friendly, very talkative.

Peter, Meg reported, had introduced her to the music of Delius, whom she'd never heard of before but was enjoying. When she and Peter listened to Delius's *Summer Night on the River*, she pretended that it was Dick who was walking together with her along the bank of the river, which was neither the river of the city in which she was stranded nor the river where he took his skinny-dips but a beautiful turquoise river that wound its way through Elysium, where she and Dick had run away. That was nice, but later in the same letter, she wrote, "I have a terrible confession to make. Peter offered me a cigarette, and I took it and smoked it. But I pretended I was sharing it with you."

Dick didn't like that, although he didn't tell Meg that he had learned to roll his own cigarettes with a can of Prince Albert and some E-Z papers. One day, in between the end of the bean-picking season and the start of the tomato-picking season, April asked Dick if he wanted to hike away back up on the mountainside to see some old Indian caves. He tried to pretend, all along the way and in the cave, that she was Meg, even when he was about to get his penis inside of her. He wrote to Meg about the Indian caves without being able to mention, or even allude to, whom he had gone there with and what they had done. Years later, he had convinced himself that if it actually had been Meg, he would not have been so nervous with her and would not have ejaculated at the moment of penetration without being able to experience the pleasure of thrusts, or if he had, Meg would have been patient with him and would have explained why that was not the way it should have gone. As it was, he thought he'd done what he was supposed to do and couldn't understand April's irritation when she said, "You aint no better than a rooster!" and would never, for the rest of that summer, let him try again.

His guilt that it was April, not Meg, kept him from feeling madly jealous when a letter came from Meg reporting that Peter had taken her to an outdoor performance of light opera in City Park. She took it upon herself to describe Peter in detail, what he wore, how tall he was, what kind of car he drove, everything. Although she insisted that, throughout the evening, she had pretended that Peter was Dick, Dick decided that she was trying to make him jealous, and he actually did scribble on a piece of writing paper, "I've got a terrible confession too. I fucked April in a cave, but I pretended it was you." He had no intention of mailing this; he just wanted to see it written out, and he burned it. In fact, he never mentioned April again in his letters to Meg, although she continued to mention Peter in all her letters to him.

V

Dick never met Peter. When Dick returned home at the end of the summer, Meg told him that Peter was gone back to the university for the fall semester, up in the Ozarks, and she didn't plan to write to him or see him again. "We had a sort of falling-out," Meg said. "Peter was just too clinging. Besides, Tata thought he was too old for me."

"So did I," Dick said. "Why did you fall out? Was he trying to get into your pants?"

"Dick!" she said. "What a thing to say." But she was blushing. After a while, she asked, "Did you try to get into April's pants?"

"I didn't just try," he blurted. "I did it."

"Oh, really?" she said. "Well, what would you think if I told you that Peter got into mine?"

"I would think you were fibbing."

"WHY WOULD IT BE A FIB FOR ME BUT NOT FOR YOU?" she wailed and started to cry but walked away from him, out of his sight, before he could watch her tears and hear her sobs.

Years later, Dick would see her again. He would have a long layover between planes in the city where she was a professor at a large university, and he would want to see her again, to reminisce about their high school years, when they scarcely ever saw each other except in passing in the hallways, had no classes together; she took three more years of Latin and was salutatorian at graduation. From the beginning of high school, where the graduates of three different junior high schools had merged together, there were plenty of kids who did not know that Meg and Dick had been outcasts and who were too worried about whether they themselves would be accepted to give any thought to whether Meg and Dick should not be accepted. In consequence of this fresh start, Meg had acquired not one girlfriend but several and was popular throughout high school and college.

She smiled when Dick reminded her of Miss Harris's ninth-grade Latin class, and she received Dick into her office for nearly two hours of talk. They were both married with children. They were both happy. It all seemed so impossibly long ago that they had known each other so dearly.

"Somewhere near my grandmother's house," Dick confessed, "there's a big old sycamore tree, and at the end of that summer, after all I'd done, I went and took my pocketknife and carved out a heart on the bark of the tree. It was an awfully lopsided heart, an irregular heart, but I put your initials and mine in it. I never got a chance to tell you that."

"So let's play 'what I'd do if I could turn the clock back,'" Meg suggested. "You can start. You wouldn't have lost your virginity to that what's-her-name? May? June?"

"April," Dick said. "No. If I could do it all over again—and I've thought about it many times—I would have seduced you one of those many afternoons we spent at your house before that summer."

"No, you wouldn't have," she said. "I couldn't have let you. I couldn't have let myself let you."

"But you let Peter," he said. "Or you claimed you did."

"There was no 'Peter,'" she said. He couldn't respond to that. He could only sit and think about it. "The heart of him I drew for you was terribly lopsided and irregular," she went on. "And if I could turn the clock back, that would be the one thing I'd change: I never would have drawn it."

A Deliberately Unambitious Divertissement

In the course of his four and a half decades as a published novelist, Donald Harington seems to have had quite a few muses. Where his great mentor and inspiration, Vladimir Nabokov, consistently dedicated his novels to his wife, Harington dedicated each of the fifteen novels published during his lifetime to a different friend, family member, or character.[1] While he did not necessarily conceive each novel with a definite dedicatee in mind, he clearly intended to use their published versions to honor specific people from his life or imagination, underscoring his conception of his books as ardent love letters to the Gentle Reader who had worn so many faces in his life.

Double Toil and Trouble (or *DUB*) makes it all sixteen Harington novels (including his nonfiction novel, *Let Us Build Us a City*) with different dedicatees, and the story behind *DUB*'s publication and its dedication to Dick McDonough only entangles the triumphs of Harington's career as a novelist still more inextricably with its tribulations. McDonough was the ardent fan who effectively rescued Harington from his mounting frustrations with both his first publisher, Random House, and his third agent, Candida Donadio, in the early 1970s. After falling in love with Stay More in *Lightning Bug*, McDonough contacted his new favorite author out of the blue and ended up bringing the huge manuscript of *Some Other Place. The Right Place.* (or *SOP. TRP.*) to Llewellyn "Louie" Howland III, editor at Little, Brown. Howland snapped up *SOP. TRP.*, and there soon

---

1. The only two exceptions to this apparent rule are the novels that Harington did not dedicate to anyone: his first published novel, *The Cherry Pit* (1965); and his first published book after his long "dark ages," the nonfiction novel *Let Us Build Us a City* (1986). Harington also published one nonfiction book during his life, *On a Clear Day: The Paintings of George Dombek* (University of Central Arkansas Press, 1995), which also carries no dedication.

began a lively and frequently urgent three-way correspondence among author, reader, and editor as Little, Brown proceeded to publish *SOP. TRP.* in 1972 and Harington's subsequent novel, *The Architecture of the Arkansas Ozarks*, in 1975.[2]

To read through Harington's letters of the first half of the 1970s (which the author carefully preserved, grouped, and archived by correspondent) is to appreciate still more the gap between the soaring ambitions of the young novelist and the humble financial realities of the young father, earnestly working to secure a place in the pantheon at the same time that he was struggling to reap something like a living from his literary labors.[3] Harington continually invokes the lofty heights to which his novels will (he is sure) elevate all three members of their privileged little coterie in the American literary marketplace, pouring out love and admiration on these readers who so loved and admired his work even as he regularly invokes the challenges that he and his family face in keeping food on the table and a home in plausible repair. But even more than the financial pressures, it is the ardent drive for close, thorough companionship that dominates these exchanges, the deaf novelist repeatedly rigging up opportunities to spend time together with his dearly beloved new friends. Promises of visits to Boston, where McDonough lived, and to Putney, Vermont, where the Haringtons lived, are interspersed with follow-up musings on the joys of the time they got to spend together and the letters their children are, with loving impatience, expecting from one another. For Harington, a literary and publishing marriage was also very much a personal one, and he pursued and celebrated such unions with the eager joy of a starry-eyed young spouse (as he would continue to do throughout his life).

In the midst of the sales figure reports and promises of visits, the letters between Harington and Howland take on a new note in early 1973. The long and richly metafictional *SOP. TRP.* was selling but not up to the author's or publisher's hopes. And that's what seems to have prompted Howland's broadly but carefully phrased request for something that eschewed the metatextual complexities of *SOP. TRP.* in favor of a

---

2. For a fuller account of Harington's frustrations with Donadio and his move, with McDonough's help, to Howland and Little, Brown, see *The Guestroom Novelist*, esp. pp. 193–96.

3. Harington was teaching art history at Windham College in Putney, Vermont, during these early years of correspondence with McDonough and Howland, but his letters strongly suggest that his day-job salary did not cover his family's needs.

straightforward narrative appropriate (as Howland put it) for Harington to give to his "maiden aunt." Within a week, Harington wrote Howland to say that he had already begun writing, in response to the broad suggestion, a novel called, initially but precisely, *For Your Maiden Aunt*. Within a couple of months, at the end of March, Harington announced that he had finished the first draft and replaced the working title with a well-known *Macbeth* allusion; a few weeks later, on April 26, 1973, he sent a clean typescript to Howland. Howland responded with praise for many elements but also with a series of questions and possible edits that would be required before he would consider publishing it with Little, Brown.[4] Faced with Howland's mixed response, Harington elected to focus on the major novel he'd already been working on, *The Architecture of the Arkansas Ozarks*, rather than investing more time in the divertissement that he had worked so hard to produce on such short notice (while teaching, no less). The author did submit *DUB* to a couple of magazines, but when they too declined it, he decided to leave it to posterity rather than trying any further to get it into print. When he refers to it a few months later in a letter to McDonough as a "rather thin work," the mild self-disparagement clearly belies the great energy and hopes that he had poured into it during its composition.

What follows below is a series of excerpts from Harington's correspondence with McDonough and Howland (along with one telling excerpt from a letter Harington wrote to his attorney, Weld S. Henshaw) that help to illuminate the origins and evolution of this long-lost Stay More novel. The dates for several of Harington's letters are conjectural, based on internal evidence and their placement in his files; in the cases where a definite date is indicated, Harington seems to have handwritten it later onto the carbon copy that he had preserved. As elsewhere, I have silently corrected typos and other obvious errors, italicized titles (which he usually underlined on his typewriter), and regularized punctuation throughout. Finally, I have retained some tidbits and grace notes from a handful of letters that, in a more general way, suggest how Harington's work on

---

4. For the full details of Howland's critique, see the Harington archive maintained by the University of Arkansas's Special Collections, which includes the original typescript of the novel with Howland's penciled comments and corrections. Among other considerations, Harington initially invited Howland to help him tweak the climax of the novel, but Howland argued for structural changes earlier in the narrative that would alter the effects of both the climax and the denouement.

DUB grew from the life and sensibilities of this most incorrigibly personal of novelists.

1. Donald Harington to Dick McDonough, ca. June 22, 1972

Thanks for your note. The jacket *is* great,[5] but I suspect the more important part is what goes on the other side of the jacket, and I hope we can get some blurbs from some influential people. Styron promises, but we'll have to wait and see . . .[6]

I agree with you, LH3 is a brilliant editor.[7] In every way, he has been just right for me, so I've got to congratulate you for finding me not only the perfect publisher but also the perfect editor. I like him so much, in fact, that I think I'll stick with him after I'm famous. Would you settle for a vice-presidency?

I wanted to invite you, Jean, and kids up for a weekend this summer [. . .].[8] Do you ever go camping? There's this Vermont state park, just a few miles from Five Corners, where we could have our picnic where a house once stood and celebrate the whole damn thing.[9]

2. Dick McDonough to Donald Harington, December 7, 1972

Fuck the *Times*.[10] There's England and [the] paperback [edition] helping out, I understand. While the critical acclaim which your talent demands has not been forthcoming, some other folks have put some money up for it. I suspect Melville's experience was not nearly as sanguine. I can only recommend my therapy for this kind of disappointment: while chopping

---

5. For Little, Brown's new edition of *Some Other Place. The Right Place.* (*SOP. TRP.*), published that same year.
6. Novelist William Styron was Harington's personal friend who had provided crucial help in getting his first novel, *The Cherry Pit* (1965), published by Random House. (See *The Guestroom Novelist*, esp. pp. 190–91.)
7. LH3 = Llewellyn "Louie" Howland III, Harington's editor for *SOP. TRP.* and *The Architecture of the Arkansas Ozarks* at Little, Brown.
8. Ellipses used to indicate an omission are bracketed in these excerpts from Harington's correspondence to distinguish them from ellipses appearing in the original texts.
9. An important setting in *SOP. TRP.*
10. James R. Frakes's mixed and frequently sarcastic review of *SOP. TRP.* had appeared in the November 12, 1972, issue of the *New York Times*.

wood against a wicked winter and just before each blow is struck, repeat the name of every major critic. [. . .]

We have added a room and a horse in Scituate. Come and see us before long.

3. Donald Harington to Dick McDonough, December 9, 1972

Yeah. Well, at least the *Times noticed* me, which is more than can be said for all other national periodicals. A silence of that magnitude can only leave me harboring sinister suspicions that there is a grand plot behind the whole thing, that *somebody* doesn't want me to be discovered.

Yet I go blithely, sanguinely on my way, concocting yet another master-work to toss into the maw of obscurity. This one, called *The Architecture of the Arkansas Ozarks*, is about six generations of the Ingledew family in mythic Stay More. Incidentally, each of the males is periodically afflicted with a terrible hereditary skin disease of the genital area, which I have chosen to call "frakes" or "the frakes." Imagine the possibilities. [. . .]

Nita and I have been thinking about doing some Xmas shopping in Boston.[11] My enthusiasm for the idea wavers from day to day, but if we do, we'll certainly seek you out.

Thanks for the words of cheer.

4. Donald Harington to Louie Howland, January 1, 1973

I have been idly speculating about what your idle speculation concerns, and while it may be speculative, it is not idle at all.[12]

5. Louie Howland to Donald Harington, January 5, 1973

My idle speculation goes something like this.

Like all major American writers, you are an overreacher. Because you have the facility to realize in words the promptings of an imagi-nation that most of us feel only in our dreams (and lose the minute we awake)—because of this facility, you are not content merely to tell a story

---

11. Nita was Harington's first wife.

12. Seemingly a reference to something in an earlier Howland letter that was not grouped with the rest of these from early 1973 that follow.

but must, rather, go beyond and outside the traditional confines of the novel-as-story.

I am more confident now than I ever was that *SOP TRIP*[13] will, sooner or later, achieve the fame and respect it deserves. But as I go through the various reviews we have had of it (too few, and few of these in any way perceptive), I do see that readers who were unable to suspend disbelief early on in this novel quickly gave up the game, so that even their praise lacked passion, whereas their blame was captious and beside the point.

These same reviewers would have reacted in just the same way to a novel by Barth or Nabokov, if Barth and Nabokov were not on their Approved List. (Approved by the Literary Mafia, of course, in return for past favors, in the time-honored fashion of Grub Street.)

How to get Donald Harington on the Approved List is our greatest challenge, I admit: our challenge collectively, yours and Little, Brown's. But I suspect that the publication of *SOP TRIP* was the most important single step we could have taken in this direction. From here on, in my view, the job is to keep publishing novels by Donald Harington, as fast as Donald Harington can write them.

Yet there are times in a writer's career when less may be more, for there is definitely a tendency among leading book reviewers (and at least some serious critics) to assume that any ambitious novel by a writer of real stature must be judged not on its own merits but within the arbitrary boundaries set by God Joyce, God Nabokov (and, latterly, God Barth and God Gass). If we could rescue you from that Procrustean bed just once, so that critics would *have* to appraise you on *your own terms*, the battle would be won.

In this context (and I might add, in this context alone), I'm inclined to believe that you might, taking a leaf from Prokofieff and his *Classical* symphony, attempt a novel that quite deliberately adheres to the traditional modes of conventional fiction. A novel, in which characters, plot, and setting are deliberately formed to create an accessible, unambiguous "story." A novel (be it [a] thriller, a comedy or tragedy, a horror or love story) that will be so unassuming in its means, so seemingly artless, that no critics may take exception to it (forget for a moment whether they actually praise it)—and which any reader of taste and moderate intelligence would want to read and recommend to maiden aunt, ailing grandparent, teen-aged daughter, or spouse.

---

13. An alternative abbreviation for *Some Other Place. The Right Place.* (*SOP. TRP.*).

Now, note. I wouldn't even mention such an idea to you, much less make a pitch to you on it, if I thought that you would actually produce a novel to these specifications. Rather, my guess is that, even if you followed this general scheme to the letter, you would find some way to sneak around the restrictions you might have consciously imposed upon such a novel. *How* you broke with the convention, without drawing attention to the breach, would be the real test of the novel's success in literary terms. (On the other hand, if it became a parody, it probably wouldn't sell too well, even if it got great reviews.)

In any event, I would rather you worked on a comparatively unambitious novel now, if you are not ready to tackle *Razorback* or *Architecture*, than to have you write short stories or even work on *A Work of Fiction* (which I want in the worst way for you to go back to one of these months or years).[14] And my reason for this is that I think you could—if you put your mind on it—disarm not only your readers but yourself with a neatly plotted, tightly drawn divertissement.

Never again should a novelist of your stature have to take the shit you had to take. I want revenge. I want you to take revenge. Now.

End of idle speculation, which, as I am sure you will agree, could hardly be idler.

6. Donald Harington to Louie Howland, January 8, 1973

Thank you for your long and historic letter, which deserves an equally long and historic reply.

I'll have to sleep on (and dream on) your idle speculation before I can fully resolve my own feelings about it, so what follows must needs be in the way of an immediate (i.e., undigested) response. I wish you would pack Jay and the kids into the VW some weekend and come up, so we could talk leisurely about such serious if idle speculations.

We are, let us admit frankly, talking from two separate angles, viz., the editor with his house's perforce pecuniary interests uppermuch, if not uppermost, and the writer with his fixed (if distorted) long-range view of

---

14. *A Work of Fiction* was the first novel that Harington completed after the publication of *The Cherry Pit*; it has never been published (see *The Guestroom Novelist*, esp. pp. 192–93). *Razorback* was a novel that Harington began work on in the late 1960s or early 1970s but never finished.

his total oeuvre. That is as it should be; if 'twere not for the one, 'twould be no the other.

Faulkner wrote *Sanctuary* as a deliberate "thriller," if we are to believe him: "the most horrible story he could think of," in reaction (reactionarily) to the public's neglect of his first five novels. It was a best seller and not a bad book, but I don't think it adds much to his stature. I have that kind of treatment projected for *The Scarlet Whickerbill* (my sixth),[15] which will tell of the relationship between Daniel Lyam Montross and his daughter Annie, but: (1) I'd rather do it after *ARK*,[16] and (2) no one could recommend it to one's maiden aunt, ailing grandparent, teen-aged daughter, or spouse.

I think possibly Nabokov had a similar intention with *Lolita*, after suffering the public's neglect of his previous six (seven? eight?) novels.

Seeing myself, as I immodestly do, somewhere between Faulkner and Nabokov, lacking the one's turgidity and the other's gamesmanship but blessed with one's sense of place and the other's love of illusions and irreality, I can't expect or entice my career, at this early point, to have a better fate than theirs had at similar points. Both were shit upon and ignored in a way far nastier than I have been lately, so I can say, while still smarting from my recent wounds, that better men than I have suffered worse.

Your and my esteemed *Sot-Weed Factor*, if I recall rightly, took about five years to get off the ground, although it may, like *SOP TRIP*, have been enjoying a 100-copy-a-week sale early in its career. Barth wrote to me, in July of '65, after I had compared him in the same nominative absolute phrase with Nabokov and Styron, "It's better, surely, to stay lean and mean through public neglect, at least in your best years, than to fall into the slackness and other misfortunes that seem to afflict the American writers we know who became very famous very early. After ten years, nobody remembers or cares about the circumstances of a book's first publicity anyhow; it's a relief, I think, when that business is over. And the less initial critical enthusiasm, the less reaction later."

He also said: "Your letter arrives as I'm finishing a novel [*Giles Goat-Boy*] that I imagine the public and critics will be even less whelmed by than they've been by its predecessors, therefore your kind words about *The Sot-Weed Factor* are gratifying."

---

15. No such novel was published or has been found among Harington's papers.
16. An alternative abbreviation (presumably) for *The Architecture of the Arkansas Ozarks* (*TAOTAO*), which Harington was working on at the time of this letter.

Two comments from me apropos our discussion: (1) Barth did not, after the initial failure of *Sot-Weed*, contemplate a more "accessible" novel but rather spent five years writing a (to me) less accessible novel, which (though I considered it a depressing failure novelistically) catapulted him onto the best-seller lists, the Approved List, and [the] Godhead (to acknowledge your so placing him, but for God's sake, please get God Gass off of there; he is, at best, Lucifer Gass).[17]

(2) If, as I am never mentally equipped to dismiss, all this world is only a solipsistic illusion, and even such atrocities as Nixon's reelection are deliberate creations of my fancy, then the public and critical acceptance (or rejection) of *SOP TRIP* is only my intended (unconsciously wished-for) plan in accordance with Barth's dictum: "It's better to stay lean and mean, etc., *at least in your best years*," etc.

I am lean. I am mean. This is my best year.

Will *Architecture* turn out to be another *Goat-Boy*? Possibly, but it seems somehow more meaningful, because more insistent, than any "conventional" fiction that I might confect or concoct, although I shall undoubtedly be prepossessed for endless hours in the weeks ahead, in sleep and awake, with ideas for a conventional, accessible novel to fit your idle speculation.[18]

But anyhow, intersession isn't long enough for me to do more than short stories. For a novel, even a conventional one, I'd have to wait for summer vacation.

Now a few bits of personal history in further substantiation of my position. Bob Loomis of Random House, as you may know, was not just overseer but gang boss and hardfisted teacher during the composition of *The Cherry Pit*.[19] One remark of his sticks with me. Early on, he said that my writing is like an "entertaining nightmare." I've never thought any of my writing is inaccessible enough to qualify as dreamlike, much less nightmarish, but that may be my lack of detachment from it. In writing *PIT*, I was like a winged horse (Mobilgas? Pegasus? What do you call them?) upon which he was an inept but tight-reining jockey. In my second novel, *Clod*, which you haven't (and shan't) read, I deliberately tried to be more conventional, down-to-earth, story oriented, and "entertaining,"

---

17. See *The Guestroom Novelist*, pp. 110 and (especially) 275.
18. On the carbon copy, Harington crossed out the last two words, "idle speculation," and wrote in "presumption."
19. Harington's first published novel (Random House, 1965).

although the plot was still too much for Loomis, while my agent Von Auw considered it "lightweight in comparison with *The Cherry Pit*," i.e., conventional, down-to-earth, story oriented, and "entertaining."[20]

Need I confess that I wrote my third novel, *A Work of Fiction*, under the spell of Barth? And that the spell was what turned both Loomis and Von Auw against me?

Lightning Bug was deliberately written as a "breather" after *A Work of Fiction*, a "comparatively unambitious" novel in which, keeping my tricks to a minimum, I stuck to a simple and, to me, conventional story. (But discovered my "postage stamp of earth" in the process.)

Razorback, of which I wrote about 80 pages last summer, was intended to be a "breather" after *SOP TRIP*, a relatively unambitious novel which anyone could understand and perhaps recommend to their maiden aunts and teen-aged sons.

As you know, I abandoned the project (the MS and all the research papers are stored away in a folder marked "R. I. P.") but learned from it a few lessons:

1. Don't write breathers. Always overreach.
2. Don't research a subject, such as football, so thoroughly that you become sick of it. (I haven't watched a single game all this season.)
3. Don't repress sexuality for the sake of maiden aunts and teen-age daughters.
4. Don't, while writing, hold your breath in expectation of imminent fame.
5. Find out how and why the Ingledews shot panthers (which I intend to do for *ARK*).
6. Cultivate your garden.

In my idle moments, lately, when I'm not writing short stories (I've done a pair of fine ones in the last week), I find myself dipping into *A Work of Fiction* for the first time in years and discovering that, just as you want in the worst way for me to go back to it, I want in the worst way for it to see the light of print.

If the reorder pattern for *SOP TRIP* keeps accelerating at its present pace, that is something we might well discuss.

---

20. For more about Harington's first agent, Ivan von Auw, see *The Guestroom Novelist*, pp. 192–93.

7. Louie Howland to Donald Harington, January 11, 1973

Your letter of January 8 is the sort of letter that editors dream about getting, but almost never do: a letter, I mean, that, when it appears in its author's collected letters or authorized biography, will instantly announce itself as being the thread through the labyrinth, the key to the lock, the fulcrum of the balance, the—dare I say it?—perkin in the velvet.[21]

Anyway, it demonstrates to me that you are in fighting trim, that you are not looking back, and that the future will be ever brighter for Donald Harington, his editor, his publisher, his readers, and the world of American letters generally.

8. Donald Harington to Louie Howland, ca. January 15, 1973

Well, confound you, I am doing it. The seed which you tossed casually into my impressionable young brain unwittingly got fertilized, and I am now 16 pages into a deliberately unambitious divertissement which came from a dream.

A few nights ago, I ran out of bourbon and had to drink Nita's scotch. (As Faulkner said, "I aint particular; between scotch and nothing, I'll take scotch."[22] I haven't fully developed my theory that we have distinctly different kinds of dreams on scotch, bourbon, and gin, but whatever the case, I woke the next day remembering the outlines of my central theme.

Pettigrew is (or was, in the '20s and '30s) the railroad terminus nearest to Stay More but still some forty miles distant. A woman debarks there, her baggage consisting of two coffins. A young man of Pettigrew, Hock Tuttle, is hired to drive her and her strange baggage to Stay More.

All of the story is seen through his eyes, and although he isn't a very curious or nosey type, undoubtedly the reader will be. I have absolutely no idea what is going to happen when they arrive at Stay More (they are still en route at page 16, where she has just had him stop the wagon in the deep woods so that he can show her how to "operate" a revolver which she has in her purse), but I have faith that my dreams will keep me filled in, from night to night.

---

21. "Perkin in the velvet" is early seventies Haringtonese for male-female sexual conjugation. (Variants of this colloquialism appear dozens of times in *SOP. TRP.*)
22. In an interview, Faulkner said, "I ain't that particular. Between Scotch and nothing, I'll take Scotch." William Faulkner, "The Art of Fiction No. 12," interview by Jean Stein, *Paris Review*, no. 12 (Spring 1956): 31, EBSCOhost.

And you, sir, shall go down in literary history, either as a perceptive editor of genius or the worst bungler of the century.[23]

9. Donald Harington to Louie Howland, ca. January 21, 1973

The untitled divertissement trips blithely along. 23 pages and I still haven't figured out what she's doing there with those two coffins. Got any ideas, smart guy?

10. Louie Howland to Donald Harington, January 26, 1973

One of the woman's coffins contains Napoleon Bonaparte's embalmed corpse. The other contains the still-warm body of a young Boston publisher. The question is: Which is which?

Anyway, I hope I haven't led you astray, and I hope you are now on page 46, at least.

11. Donald Harington to Louie Howland, ca. January 28, 1973

I stopped at page 44 to read your letter urging me to page 46. Don't crowd me, man.

This is great fun, at least. And while it may be deliberately unambitious, it fills in some history of the Ingledew saga and is therefore relevant to *Architecture*.

12. Donald Harington to Louie Howland, February 10, 1973

I seem to be doing things in ten-year cycles, since *For Your Maiden Aunt* (as we shall tentatively call it) was commenced exactly ten years to the month since I commenced *The Cherry Pit*, which is also ten years to the month since my first Little, Brown rejection slip.

13. Donald Harington to Louie Howland, ca. February 18, 1973

Classes have resumed at Windham, which is slowing down *For Your Maiden Aunt*, but I'm working weekends on it. It's at least as good as *True Grit*, which I've never got over envying the success of, since I went

---

23. Harington signed this letter "Divertissemently yours."

to college with the author, and it's considered, generally, as Arkansas's finest novel.

14. Donald Harington to Dick McDonough, ca. February 20, 1973[24]

On the first anniversary of historic events perpetrated by you on my behalf, greetings, felicitations, and remembrances.

You aren't Vice-President yet, and I'm not on the NYTBSL yet, but we haven't lost any ground. At least I haven't. How about you? You've got a horse now, and I'm trading in my Volvo for a Chevrolet Blazer (4-wheel drive).

Louie [Howland] may have told you of his Grand Scheme for licking the jinx that hovers over me. As a result, I'm now writing a "deliberately unambitious divertissement," a thriller. The critics won't know what to make of it. Neither will I, for that matter.

Don't tell him I said so, but I think what Louie really has in mind is a demonstration that, if I can't be the next Nabokov, I'll be the next Graham Greene.

Well hell, they both made the same amount of money, but Greene had his to spend earlier. I don't like Swiss hotels anyway.[25]

It takes a couple of months to get a Blazer delivered, and this Volvo is falling apart day by day, so we'll come and ride your horse just about the time he's grazing the first grass.

15. Donald Harington to Louie Howland, ca. March 21, 1973

I'm tempted to send you the rough first draft of *For Your Maiden Aunt*, but I don't believe in showing unfinished and unpolished work, so I can't. Nor do I believe in rushing things. So I'll have it ready when it's ready. Meanwhile, if you see a dollar lying around loose, put your foot on it.

------

24. Harington seems to have signed a contract with Little, Brown for *SOP. TRP.* between an anxiously hopeful letter he wrote to McDonough on February 15, 1971, and an exuberantly celebratory follow-up dated February 27, 1972, which concludes with the sentence, "*Thanks* is a tiny, impotent, impoverished word."

25. A reference to Nabokov's final residence, the Montreux Palace hotel in Montreux, Switzerland, where he famously lived (after the massive success of *Lolita* had made him financially independent) from the early 1960s until his death in 1977.

16. Donald Harington to Louie Howland, March 31, 1973

It is done. Your deliberately unambitious divertissement is completed, complete with actual, untentative title, *Double Toil and Trouble* (no ambiguous comment on the effort of writing or reading it). . . . [I]t will sell quite readily to Hollywood and make us all rich.

I'll have a final draft typed up and sent to you in time for you to peruse it at leisure and perhaps return it in person when you and Jay come up some weekend in April. (Any weekend; take your pick; we're always here, can't afford to go anywhere.)

Always after completion of a book, I go into a blue funk, probably because no book of mine has ever turned out to be what I originally intended it to be. That is less so in the case of *Double*, but I've still been in a funk.

My hair and beard are turning gray; I have no doubt that *Double* will bail us out, by and by, but that is weeks ahead, and my creditors are getting nasty. Could you beg, borrow, or embezzle a reasonable approximation of what I might later be entitled to? Thanks.

17. Donald Harington to Louie Howland, April 20, 1973

This thank-you note must needs be in haste, as I am up to my ass in typewriter work with the final draft of *Double Toil* but want you to know the check arrived in the nick (or gash) of time to get the creditors' collective feet out of the door.

We look forward to entertaining you and Jay on the 5th of May. (Daniel Lyam M. didn't write that rhyme. [And the 4th and 6th of May too.])[26] I will be mailing aforementioned *Toil* to you next week.

18. Donald Harington to Louie Howland, April 26, 1973[27]

Job ORDER

HARINGTON LITERARY FABRICATIONS LTD.

Customer: Llewellyn Howland III

---

26. Brackets in original.
27. Apparently a cover sheet for the typescript of *DUB*.

Job: One (1) deliberately unambitious divertissement which adheres to the traditional modes of conventional fiction, so unassuming in its means, so seemingly artless, that no critics may take exception to it, and which any reader of taste and moderate intelligence would want to read and recommend to maiden aunt, ailing grandparent, teen-aged daughter, or spouse.

Delivered: April 26, 1973

19. Donald Harington to Louie Howland, ca. May 1, 1973

You have the first sheet of my new stationery. You should also have, by now, the first and second sheets of my new novel.

I am not satisfied with the *deus ex McKinna*, but why deprive a nice editor of a little work? Together, we can sew a few threads hither and yon.

Just as Buddy Portis wrote *True Grit* with John Wayne in mind as the star, I wrote *Double Toil* with Joanne Woodward in mind. But I won't quibble too much if Liz Taylor grabs the property.

We hope all things are favorable for you to head our way this weekend.

20. Donald Harington to Weld S. Henshaw,[28] ca. May 8, 1973

At the suggestion of Louie and Dick McDonough, I have just finished a new novel called *Double Toil and Trouble*, which, according to Louie's prescription, is a "deliberately unambitious divertissement," a "thriller," if you will. Since Louie ordered it, he can't very well turn it down, but I think it's good enough to make it on its own, and the advance on that book will finally put me in the black. What's more, it's a surefire Hollywood property.

We're looking forward to warm weather and a trip to Maine.

21. Donald Harington to Dick McDonough, ca. July 1973

I haven't heard from you in a coon's age.

It's a good summer up this way; my garden is more productive than ever, and so is my pen: I'm well into my epic examination of the arcane

---

28. Harington's attorney.

architecture of the Arkansas Ozarks. Louie will get the first batch next week in my hopes for a contract; it's the old story: no cash and many bills.

There was a rather thin work I completed, having to do with twin coffins, a young man, and a woman no longer young, which fizzled at Little, Brown but is under serious consideration at *Redbook* magazine, and even if they reject it, I can still cannibalize it in some future installment of the ongoing Stay More saga.

Let's visit one of these days, one direction or the other.

Sources

Harington, Donald. *Double Toil and Trouble*, 1973. Special Collections, University of Arkansas.

————. "Down in the Dumps." *Esquire*, February 1967.

————. "The Freehand Heart," ca. 1995. Special Collections, University of Arkansas.

————. "A Second Career." *Esquire*, January 1967.

————. "Telling Time." In *Yonder Mountain: An Ozarks Anthology*, edited by Anthony Priest. Fayetteville, AR: University of Arkansas Press, 2013.